MURIEL

by George P. Elliott

AMONG THE DANGS

CONVERSIONS

FROM THE BERKELEY HILLS

DAVID KNUDSEN

AN HOUR OF LAST THINGS

IN THE WORLD

MURIEL

PARKTILDEN VILLAGE

A PIECE OF LETTUCE

MURIEL

a novel by

GEORGE P. ELLIOTT

E. P. DUTTON & CO., INC · NEW YORK · 1972

The author wishes to thank the John Simon Guggenheim
Foundation and the Corporation of Yaddo for their generous
help in making time and space available for
the writing of much of this book.

*The Woman in This Story
Loved Her Husband, Whose Love
for Her Soured, and Her Children,
Who Turned from Her.*

MURIEL

1

Maiden

Muriel's mother, her father's mother, and her widowed sister were altos in the choir of Trinity Episcopal Church. Muriel's voice was rather thin, but after a year in Wichita, in Miss Turner's School for Young Ladies, where she studied voice, she dared join the choir too. At first she was afraid she might disgrace her folks. Her mother stood on one side of her, her sister and grandmother on the other, singing strong, smiling at her from time to time. All four Storr women were buxom and quite short; they wore well-starched white dresses, their hair wound in buns on top of their heads. In less than a month Muriel's fledged alto was soaring with theirs.

Before Halloween that year, the choirs of nine churches in Ames, even the Friends' Meeting, joined to rehearse *The Messiah* two nights a week, for performance on Christmas Eve in the high school gymnasium. The first evening, as she was standing there all keyed up and unready, there rang in her ears the tenor recitative. The singer was a spare, straight young man, and the proud way he cocked his head when he sustained a note made her hold her own head that same way, and her lips shadowed his. He had a long neck, and once she caught herself half-mesmerized watching his Adam's apple as he sang. He did not modulate gracefully as she knew she could teach him to, but plunged loud to soft, soft to loud. His hands were weathered, he wore work shoes. She did not ask her family who he was, but instead asked Mona, a Unitarian girl with a withered arm, whom she made a point of being good to. Mona, thrilled to be in on things, asked Paul, a Presbyterian baritone; he told them to go ask his aunt, the harmonium player. First she puckered her lips at Muriel, then she winked and whispered. The tenor was Ed Bell, a Baptist from Dunreith four miles east of Ames, and he farmed with his father—corn, wheat, and hogs, with a few milch cows. This was as bad as Muriel had feared (her father was the town dentist and they usually had the richest man in Ames to Thanksgiving dinner). Maybe she didn't want to improve Ed's singing as much as all that.

Just before the next rehearsal, as she was chatting with Mona over among the sopranos, she caught Ed's eyes resting on her. Their coolness troubled her. She blushed, and turned. Giggling, Mona nudged her. He was starting to come toward them. She hurried to the alto section and took her place, in front of her mother, between her sister and her grandmother. She did not feel him look at her again that night, to her relief—nor during the next practice either, to her pique.

The Saturday after Thanksgiving they practiced in the afternoon and then had a potluck supper in the Methodist Church basement. The Storrs brought chicken and dumplings, which Muriel dished up. Ed came for seconds before she'd served herself, and asked her if she had cooked the stew.

"I helped Mama. Is it good?"

He didn't even smile, just nodded and walked off.

Well then! He needed a lesson, a sharp one, and not a singing lesson either. Mona had saved a place at table for Muriel—but right next to *him*. She tried to edge Mona over by him, but Mona got cross and wouldn't budge. He was watching.

"Set down," he said. "My name's Ed Bell."

12

She did not answer, and sat down.

"That's better," he said.

"Mr. Bell, anyone with your voice should sing much better than you do."

He sized her up. "Is that a fact?"

"Did you ever have voice lessons?"

"Well, not exactly. Munt Bryant taught me a good deal—anyway, all I ever got taught."

"Who's he?"

"Our blacksmith out at Dunreith. He's the best singer I ever heard. Not that I've been very far."

"Why isn't he singing with us?"

"Yes," said Mona, "why isn't he? Didn't anybody ever ask him?"

"No," said Ed, "he's a Catholic."

"Even so," said Muriel, frowning, "if he's that good, I don't see why we shouldn't ask. There's nothing wrong with him, is there?"

He stopped eating and looked at her hard. "You must be Episcopal."

"We are Episcopalians, *sir*, and what difference does that make?"

"Maybe," said Mona soothingly, "his priest won't let him sing with us. They don't, you know. That's what I've heard."

"No, ma'am," said Ed, "you could hardly say he's got a priest—thirty miles to Beulah Center. He goes Easters." He turned back to Muriel. "I'd heard there's a lot you Episcopals don't know. I see there is, all right."

"And what, *if* I may ask, is funny about inviting somebody to help us sing the best music in the whole world?"

"Well, ma'am, some of my Baptist kin are mad at me for being here with all you denominations, and now you ask why Catholics aren't here."

"But you're a friend of his!"

"I'm funny that way."

"Well," she said, "I may not know so much, but I could teach you something anyhow."

13

"Is that so?" he said calmly.

"If I felt like it. I studied voice in Wichita."

"Well, yes, indeed. It'd be generous of you to show me how to breathe right. Munt don't know how but he said it was important. He never had lessons either. Still, when the weather's warm enough to leave doors open and Munt feels good, everybody in Dunreith hears how good he feels and they feel the better for it. I'd like that."

"Oh, you are so right!" When he laughed she noticed that his teeth were bad. She leaned forward toward him, her hands clasped under her chin. "My daddy's the dentist."

Ed's face closed.

"Oh, now, I didn't mean to hint. I help him around the office. It's just off the dining room."

Mona smiled across Muriel anxiously. "I'll go get you some pumpkin pie, Ed."

Muriel offered a quick prayer that, while Mona was gone, he'd make up. "If you'd like me to teach you how . . . If you'd like to learn to breathe right . . ."

"Thanks, ma'am, some day I surely would. But this twice a week rehearsing takes all my spare time. We get up by five o'clock. The first time I missed prayer meeting, Ma cried."

"Whenever you can, I'd love to. Later on?"

"I'll keep that in mind."

One week he missed both practice nights. Paul's aunt told Mona he had sick headaches.

"Of course," said Muriel, giving her head an angry shake, "with such teeth. But he won't listen."

"Yes," Mona sighed, "what can you do with a stubborn man?"

Muriel, hearing too much sympathy in Mona's voice, glanced at her sharply; her mouth was puckered down, but her eyes were keen.

"Poor Muriel, I know how you feel."

"There's nothing wrong with him that Dad can't fix," Muriel said, and smiled past Mona's shoulder as though someone had

14

caught her eye. She went over to Miss Whitcomb, gave her a nice pat, and asked how her aged father's hip was mending.

At the "Hallelujah Chorus," even though she loved singing it, she slipped off to go home early, waving her forefinger at Mona, giving her head a pert shake and shrugging a little, as though these signals would explain her leaving early when of course they only added to the mystery; she was not just avoiding Mona but leaving her there high, dry, and worried.

She decided to take it easy with Ed, but she hardly had a chance to do even that. After the potluck supper, he only spoke to her about unimportant things—the weather, mostly, on and on about the weather. He never sought her out except, sometimes, with his eyes, his dark, steady eyes. On Christmas Eve during the performance, she could not help listening with fresh ears, and it pained her to hear how crude he sounded beside Sven Larsson; Sven had nothing like as fine a voice as Ed, but he'd studied in Kansas City and knew what to do with it.

Homeward, huddling behind their two men against the arctic wind, the Storr women chattered along the broad right-angled streets of Ames. The wind blew hard enough to bang loose gates; it keened at eaves. The huge sky had been frozen clean. On their front walk Muriel's father stopped them and reached his arms up, preparing them for a quotation: "For God so loved the world!" He usually quoted Shakespeare, but this was a more Biblical occasion. "My cup runneth over," he said.

In bed, she thought about Ed's voice. "Such a beautiful natural instrument, just going to waste!" Tears filled her eyes. Her mother, not yet calmed down from the performance, came in to kiss her good night and was alarmed to find her wiping her eyes. Muriel said things had just been too much—the decorations, the bright sky, *The Messiah*, all too lovely. She almost told her ·about Ed; but not quite. Her mother pressed Muriel's head against her bosom and called her her mouse; then ran down to the Christmas tree where the white presents were heaped high to be opened after breakfast, and "stole" treats from Muriel's stocking, two pieces of divinity for her dear mouse to nibble on. "But,

15

Mother," she felt like saying, "I'm no longer a child. I'm a woman in love." Still, she said the candy was delicious and let her mother rub her head.

Bob Roberts, who owned the Dry Goods Emporium, had bought the first automobile in Briggs County a few years before. Everybody had expected one of the two leading citizens to get the first machine; but Mort Raleigh (the one the Storrs had to Thanksgiving dinners) was a miserly old bachelor, and Oval Tomlinson, bank president and Knight Templar, said he'd buy the first machine he saw that was half, just half, as handsome as his team of matched bay stallions and he sure had not seen it yet. It was generally allowed that Bob Roberts was maybe a little sporty, but he was a widower and he wasn't reaching above himself. He had made a lot of jokes about his Stanley Steamer, called it a money-breathing dragon, a white elephant, a shandy dancer.

Early in the spring after *The Messiah*, Bob Roberts came to have Mr. Storr fit him for false teeth. Muriel was in the office at the time, being her father's assistant, and she overheard Bob Roberts tell how his son Robbie had got in a fight with Ed Bell Saturday night at a barn dance where Ed was the caller. Ed was so good at seven-up he had played in the east Kansas championship finals; at the dance Robbie got him to play for matches; there was a jug of corn liquor; he'd skunked Robbie, and then . . . Muriel ran from the office to her room and threw herself across the bed. Even there, she heard their laughter; she pressed her hands over her ears. Corn liquor! How could she ever have let such a lowlifer fool her? Gambling for money! She would put Ed Bell out of her mind, she would cease to think about him.

And she did, that very minute.

She went about humming, "I'll make the punishment fit the crime." The year before at Miss Turner's, she had played Pooh-Bah in *The Mikado;* she didn't have the voice for the part, of course, but everybody agreed she was very expressive. "The punishment fit the crime," she sang aloud. Her father looked at her quizzically, and she ran out tittering like the three little maids from school.

16

She busied herself in the young people's group at church: wienie roasts, Thursday socials, charity bazaars, sewing bees. The boys were healthy-minded and the girls good-hearted. She never took an active part in Job's Daughters, though she had to join because her father was a thirty-third-degree Mason. Up-and-coming young men in Ames joined the Masons but did not look to Job's Daughters for wives especially. Muriel thought that the church group had a much livelier spirit.

After they'd been on a hayride once with the Senior Epworth League (Methodist), they went to Robbie Roberts's house and bobbed for apples and even played post office; three boys kissed her, and Roy McNeil kissed her nine times. She began knitting baby clothes for two girls from Miss Turner's; they had married brothers, so they'd had a double wedding. Around the house she made a point of singing at least once a day; her father called her his warbler. What made her happiest was that her mother would ask her advice on handling Dick, her fifteen-year-old brother, who wanted to quit going to high school; they kept him in.

Roy McNeil, the undertaker's son, sat by her at church; she liked him, though it was said he smoked cigars and had been known to play poker for money. That fall when she heard that Ed had gone to Topeka to Baptist missionary school, she felt a small pang. On New Year's Day, Roy proposed.

She put him off till May, to see if she could ever bring herself to love him. On Valentine's Day an envelope with just her name on it appeared in the mailbox; between the blue hearts, in Roy's hand, there was a sonnet; the first letters of the lines, in large red capitals, spelled ILOVEYOU MURIEL. She had sent him a printed Valentine, unsigned, and written his address with her left hand; but he told her he knew right away that she'd sent it, because even left-handed she made the dots over the i's in little unclosed circles. She liked it that he'd studied her so closely. She told him his poem was lovely. In May she said to wait till the end of June.

Her father sprained his shoulder spading the garden back by the alley. Muriel jumped at the chance to help, digging and hoeing furiously, sowing vegetable seed galore. Her father urged her not to work too hard, and her mother told her it looked peculiar for a young lady to be working a vegetable patch; a bed of flowers would look better. "But, Mama, our own taste so good!" She liked fresh green beans, tomatoes, acorn squash, onions, sweet corn; besides, it tickled her to see old ladies elevate their eyebrows. But mostly she was enjoying (though she never mentioned it aloud) the new ache of muscles, the still of body at day's end, feeling herself everywhere pierced by the bright, dry air, her tingling flesh aching, alive clear through.

In June she went to West Beulah to serve as one of the bridesmaids for a forty-second cousin Rosemary Stonehouse, her best friend from Miss Turner's. The wedding was to be in St. Bartholomew's Episcopal Church, which had twelve stained-glass windows made in Belgium and a crucifix of pure silver. Muriel knew their church in Ames was lower than her mother would have preferred. "We're low church, but praise God, we don't have to have a Ladies' Aid." Even at Miss Turner's, where a big point was made of doing things right, *priest* was for Roman Catholics. She had heard Baptists and such call their *minister* a *preacher*. But she hardly knew what to think when Mr. and Mrs. Stonehouse referred to their Dr. Wrigley as a *priest*.

Were the Stonehouses trying to be daring, or what? Suppose communion turned out to be in Latin? How would she know when to kneel? It made her so nervous, thinking of this, that she almost asked Rosemary about it. But she told herself severely that she must not upset a bride with her own petty worries. She'd just watch what the others did and follow along—the way Miss Turner said she had done when she had attended church services in Italy. Imagine, going abroad to West Beulah! The notion tickled Muriel so much she felt a lot better about things.

Mr. Stonehouse, a prosperous businessman, was giving the newlyweds a house in California; there Rosemary's husband-to-be, Preston McPherson, would go into partnership with his Uncle Rupert as a certified public accountant.

Mrs. Stonehouse kept announcing she was not going to break down once; but as soon as Rosemary put her veil on, her mother

18

quaked, and when Rosemary stood by the front door with the bouquet of pink rosebuds at her bosom, Mrs. Stonehouse cracked, gasping rigidly. Muriel offered to hug her; she glared; Muriel hugged her anyway, and she collapsed on her shoulder. Rosemary's lips began trembling. Muriel made a little sign to frowning Mr. Stonehouse; he rushed Rosemary out to the touring car. Presently Mrs. Stonehouse pulled herself together, wiped her eyes, tucked in her hair, and thanked Muriel with a wordless squeeze of the hand.

In the vestibule of the church, they took their places for the wedding procession. An usher opened the main door. A male quartette was finishing a number.

Again the bugle of Ed's unmistakable voice pierced her. Her hands clapped over her ears, as they'd done since her childhood whenever she was startled; but right away she spread her fingers a little, peeking as it were to hear him. She felt herself blush, but luckily no one was paying attention to her.

Then the organ made her march in, with downcast eyes, as a bridesmaid should. Twice during the ceremony she feared that her knees would buckle. Despite her fixed smile, her lips trembled. Dr. Wrigley in his lace cuffs and collar, the way he said *Gahd* instead of plain *God*, the incense visible in the shafts of stained morning sunlight, so many candles (thank the Lord, there was no Latin)—she was grateful to feel Ed's familiar eyes on her during the service. Her heart flowed over.

Muriel had been looking forward to the wedding party (they called it a "reception") almost as much as to the wedding itself. The Stonehouses had hired a maid and butler (a Negro couple, with a truck patch near Beulah Center, who hired themselves out for functions) to serve open-faced sandwiches, fruit punch, Neapolitan ice cream squares, and of course pieces of the snowy-white five-tiered cake. Whispering in bed the night before, Rosemary had said her father had three bottles of French champagne with corks that bulged like toadstools, all covered with a lattice-work of fine wires; he wanted to gather the men by the swing in the grape arbor and drink a toast to the bridegroom; her mother would not hear of such a thing; they would have to drink it in

19

the dining room with the doors shut, so the children would not know.

The party turned out to be everything it should be: the children were pretty as little angels, the groom's face wore a silly grin, all the women had on white gloves, Rosemary was radiant, nothing went wrong, the dogs did not even get through the garden gate and make a commotion. Carl Fliegel, the best man, was very attentive to Muriel. He was an up-and-coming farm equipment sales manager for central Kansas, and Rosemary said she happened to hear her father tell her uncle that last year Carl had made over two thousand dollars.

Even so, Muriel was not as happy as she wanted to be, because of Ed. She was bothered that Ed *Bell* was a member of a quartette the name of which was the *Morgan* Brothers Quartette. But more important, listening to them sing jaunty spirituals while the guests were coming from church, to hear them harmonizing while man and wife as one held the handle of the knife and gave the cake the first cut, she could not help learning with a twinge how handsomely Ed was singing now. He must have studied voice. Later on when she saw the quartette joining the party, she went over to Rosemary's great-grandmother in the arbor seat and began saying things to her through her ear trumpet, so as to discourage Ed, just in case.

When she went back for seconds on the ice cream and cake, she overheard two respectable-looking men with cigars between their fingers.

"I don't suppose anybody's giving the kids a shivaree."

"Phil and Barney talked about it."

"Remember the great one we gave Achilles and Mary Catherine? They didn't get to bed till dawn."

"And tired! We kept Kill in a duck blind over at Tuckarora Pond for an hour or two before he got away—swam across, a good quarter of a mile. Well, but they've come up in the world."

She was shocked a little; in Ames, respectable people at a wedding would not even talk about shivarees anymore; at least, she had never heard anybody do it. Despite appearances, West Beulah must be somewhat lax.

Mr. Stonehouse waved the men toward the house (for the champagne!) Ed went in without having spoken to her. Good. But she kept an eye out. When she saw the other men return to the garden and heard a whinny, a "Giddap!," and wheels on the gravel, she ran to the corner of the house and watched a buckboard with the quartette in it trotting down the lane. Ed looked back; she could have sworn he saw her; she started to lift her hand, but he didn't wave; she let her hand fall.

When the newlyweds ran through the hails of rice to the machine that Preston's brother had lent them for the occasion, Muriel shrieked loudest. As they rattled off with a string of tin cans tied to the axle she half-broke down, smiling through her sniffles. Rosemary had confided they were going to stay in a Wichita hotel that night and next morning catch the train for California. It was the most romantic thing that had ever happened to Muriel. When Carl gave her his monogrammed handkerchief to blow her nose on, she thanked him, but she could not look at him. Her feelings were too precious to be shared, by even so much as a glance, with anybody but her most intimate friend.

The next Sunday afternoon, Roy McNeil took her on a picnic, just the two of them. She felt funny about it because Roy's mother wouldn't even let her devil some eggs but insisted everything had to be a surprise; the only surprise Muriel could see was a whole roasted pullet, but it was so underdone her cheeks ached with smiling how good it was and making up compliments for Roy to pass on to his mother. They were sitting on the bank of Indian Creek about a mile east of town, under a shady elm; there weren't too many ants or flies; there was no wind, so there wasn't any dust in the air. The swale might have looked very romantic if she hadn't known where it was, in Sawyer Lamb's back forty which she had known about all her life. Just as Roy began holding her hand, half a dozen milch cows came down to the creek to drink, and before he'd said anything, what little romantic atmosphere there was left was destroyed by gnats, which she had to use her free hand to wave off. He proposed again; she said yes.

21

That night in bed, the chief thing she thought about was whether she would do what she ought if Carl Fliegel should ever call. At least he was a Mason, like her father, instead of an Odd Fellow, like Roy and his father. Carl did call, the next week: she did her duty and sent him away.

Her mother told her to be sensible and not rush things with Roy, but even her mother was taken aback when she didn't set the date before next May. Muriel insisted that she wanted to be married on Mother's Day—they owed their mothers *that* much. Everybody "looked at her cross-eyed," in her father's expression, about the Mother's Day idea—except Roy, who thought it was a sweet thought and let her have her way. She was so fond of him. Her father said Yes, he'd prefer it if Roy was a Mason instead of an Odd Fellow but there was no use getting upset about it, time would tell, things change. Roy was a good man. He went to church. He did not drink, gamble, or use vulgar language in her presence. He liked to do homey things; he would sit in the kitchen cracking walnuts while she made fudge, and when she gave him an extra piece when no one was looking, a *bonus*, he would kiss her and squeeze her arm.

Hard as she tried, she could not put it out of her mind that he was an undertaker. His ailing father would not let go of the business, though Roy actually did everything. Occasionally he wanted to tell her something interesting that had happened on the job, but she would not let him even though he swore it was in good taste. Once he told her that the winter he'd been in the eighth grade Ed Bell was his father's assistant embalmer. That was the terrible winter of the smallpox epidemic, the one in which Muriel's brother-in-law and her two aunts had died. Mr. McNeil had been stricken; Roy said his father liked to boast they'd dug his grave and picked out the headstone for it, but look how he'd fooled them. She pumped Roy to tell her everything that had happened that winter. The key to it all, Roy said, as far as they were concerned, was Ed. He had come through like a prince till spring, but then he'd had to go back to the farm; his father had a rupture, and his brothers were too little to be much help; nothing ever came of Ed's career as an undertaker. She liked the word *mortician*, but she couldn't get Roy to use it; he said there weren't many things he was stubborn about but that was one of them. It was that night she made him promise never to mention undertaking to her again, the details of it. After he had kept his promise for three months, she began to feel sure of him. In mid-October, they told their best friends they would announce their engagement on New Year's Day.

Sometimes Muriel's mind, when a word like *shit* dropped into it, would revolve the foreign object for a while; but then, finding no sustenance in it, would let it plop out; nothing had happened. Once when she was thirteen, she had flinched from her father's fingers gently stroking her arm because she had suddenly imagined them probing inside wide-open, drooling mouths. She put this image out of her mind fast, and squirmed against him on the sofa, guiding his hand to her brown hair. When she was with Roy, she worked to keep thoughts of funerals out of her mind; however, she neglected to guard against corpses, never having seen one. Once when he was silently rubbing her forehead and lightly drawing his fingertips over her eyelids, there dropped into her mind the picture of his fingers closing the eyelids of a corpse flat on its back in a casket; with a whimper, she jerked from him and shook her head hard to get the image out of it. Then she saw the bewilderment in his eyes and feared it would turn to pain. She murmured that she loved him so much and guided his gentle fingers to her neutral hair.

The Messiah two years before had gone so well that the combined choirs decided to sing *Elijah*. People said it was too Old Testament for Christmas, so it was set for New Year's Eve. The first week of rehearsal, Judge Reidenbaugh bleated the tenor; but then, to everybody's relief, he begged off, saying he was too busy with some unexpected cases. Paul's aunt, the harmonium player, came to Dr. Storr on Monday to have a tooth filled, and told Muriel a delegation of five had gone out to Ed and begged him on bended knee to be the tenor soloist. They agreed to change rehearsals from Tuesday and Friday nights to Monday and Thursday, so he could sing with the Morgan Quartette whenever they got weekend jobs.

23

"Ed *Bell?*" Muriel said. "The *Morgan* Quartette?"

Paul's aunt said that Ed's oldest sister was married to one of the three Morgan brothers, so he was at least a Morgan brother-in-law. That might be stretching a point, but while as a trio they'd done fair, as a quartette they were the most asked-for in twelve counties, occasionally even as far up as Nebraska; Ed made all the difference.

At his first rehearsal he sang so well Muriel fell to wondering again what he might do with *professional* training. From where she stood in the front row of the altos, facing Mona, she saw him in profile. Singing purged his expression of its sternness, but the cock of his head was arrogant as ever. When his voice soared out over all the others, she lost herself. She felt it was wonderfully honest of him not to rise up on his toes when reaching for the high notes, but to keep his feet squarely planted when he stretched to full height.

At the rest pause, she found herself wishing Roy was in the choir too. (She'd asked him to join, but he snorted; singing was for birdies. She thought he said it to impress her father, who was no singer either; at the time, they were out on the porch swing, Muriel between the two men fanning off the smoke from their cigars; Roy leaned forward and caught a smile from Dr. Storr.) Roy might not be too exciting but he always made her feel safe. Not, for goodness' sake, that she was in danger now, with her folks around her, the choirs, so many girl friends.

Mona sought her out to tell her that during Ed's solo she'd looked as though she were hearing angels; Mona said she'd had a great-aunt Phoebe Lulax who had often heard angel voices in her old age, she'd lived to be eighty-seven; her face looked *so* lovely when she was listening to them, just like Muriel's when Ed was singing. Muriel felt as though her soul was being splashed with wet cornmeal mush. On the spot she resolved to be excruciatingly "nice" to Mona. When Ed came up to them, she held Mona's useless arm and told him how wonderfully Mona was overcoming her handicap. Apparently she did not gush enough: Ed was very kind and Mona beamed. Muriel bit the inside of her lower lip; she would have to be "nicer" yet, if she was to keep

24

that wet mush scraped off. Then, seeing the gentleness in their eyes, she was ashamed of her mean impulse. She ran to the vestry room and hid behind the coats to cry. Mona came looking for her, calling, "Muriel, is something the matter?" She buried her sobs in a scarf till Mona went away without finding her.

It began to seem that everywhere she turned she saw Ed or heard people mention him. In the hardware store she found him buying chicken wire and staples; they chatted for a few minutes; he said he was going to be caller at a Thanksgiving dance in Bettancourt, and she said she'd never been to a barn dance; half-squinting, he began twiddling the end of his nose with his forefinger; she was going to toss her head at him for being impertinent, but he winked in such a droll way she collapsed into giggles and ran out of the store. He was the tri-county champion that year at clipping briar hedgerow, half a rod more than next best; she heard Bob Roberts boast that Ames had cause to be proud of Ed Bell. ("But he's really from Dunreith!" she felt like saying.) At Mr. Whitcomb's funeral Ed was the soloist, and Roy invited him home to supper; she was trying to decide whether she ought to go to Roy's house for supper too— but he didn't even ask her. She could hardly help noticing what naturally good manners Ed had, much better than Roy's. Once in a while, though, Ed would do something surprisingly crude such as belch in front of ladies; a lapse, nothing more; all it meant was that he needed some polishing, a woman's touch; he'd probably been too much for his mother, poor woman, she'd been overworked all her life.

One cold evening after rehearsal he crooked his arm for her and said he was walking her home. If he'd asked her whether he might, she would have known how to say no. If he had taken her arm first, she would have given him such a look! But he did not pick up the hints she dropped, held his arm for her to take, firmly, crudely, politely, and waited. She cast a lifeline look to her mother, who just smiled. She wished her grandmother was still singing. (She'd lost her voice that summer, with the quinsy.) *She* would have come to the rescue.

"Let's go," he said. Blushing, she put her arm through his.

25

They went home roundabout. She kept looking for exactly the right moment to mention casually that she was engaged. It failed to present itself.

If he wasn't going to make conversation, she had to. "Ed, are you an Odd Fellow?"

He glared at her. "What in the name of Hannah gave you that idea?"

"Oh, I don't know, I was just wondering what lodge you belong to."

"My sister Ethel is a maiden in the Minnehaha chapter of the Pocahontas branch of the women's auxiliary of the Improved Order of Red Men." He laughed, but it was more like a bark than a laugh. "Hell, I'm not even a Moose."

"Ed!" Such disrespectful language! Why was he so upset all of a sudden?

"I apologize." The expression on his face remained very sour.

"I should just think so." She gave his forearm a forgiving little squeeze—through his coat sleeve, of course, with her gloves on, not too forward. "Daddy's a Mason."

"If I was to be anything, I'd be a Mason. They take care of their own."

"Daddy says there never has been a President who wasn't a Mason, and there never will be."

"I suppose."

When they got to her house, she did not invite him in. He did not seem to know how to say good night; he just stood there on the front steps holding both her hands in both his; finally he squeezed so hard she cried out, "Ouch, you're awfully strong." He scowled at her tenderly, then walked off blowing in his gloves.

"Marry him?" she whispered in bed. "It's ridiculous. I'm engaged. Of course, I don't have a ring yet. But what would Mama say? He's nothing but a dirt farmer." She shivered down farther under the covers. "He's so independent. But does he have to be so crude? The first thing I'd do is make him let Daddy fix his teeth. All those sick headaches—so unnecessary."

Powerful, vague sensations rose from her womb. She thought

26

of cuddling and nursing her baby, Roy's precious firstborn. She curled on her left side in bed so the baby boy might rootle at her breast freely, and she loosened the covers the better to watch his dear face. She gasped. In the pitch black under the covers she saw that her darling boy's eyes weren't blue and bulging like Roy's but brown and deep-set like Ed's. She pulled the covers tight around her neck and squeezed her eyes tight. She knew how silly she was being, but she couldn't get that face out of her mind. It wasn't really a baby's face at all, and it certainly didn't belong on *her* baby. She could not help making huge, hiccuping, dry sobs.

When she heard her mother's footsteps coming down the hall, Muriel took hold of herself. She said she'd just been having a bad dream. Clucking, her mother sat on the edge of the bed and patted her, as she had done when Muriel was little; at least she did not offer to fetch her some peanut brittle from the big jar that was always stocked for "special occasions." Still, when her mother stood in the doorway blowing a good-night kiss, Muriel knew it would make her mother happy to be asked to do her a little favor. She asked her for a piece to go to sleep on. What if she was too heavy? She could tell by the way her mother clasped her hands under her chin and said, "Oh yes," how good it made her feel; one of the little things, as Grandfather Storr used to say, that count for so much in this life. Anyway, she *liked* peanut brittle.

The first Monday in December Ed told her that that Saturday there was to be a barn dance near Dunreith, with a barbecued hog, corn bread, buttered yams, sour apple pie, cake, and a taffy pull maybe, though they weren't sure about that yet, with the best dancer being awarded a live turkey at the end of the evening. Ed was going to be one of two callers. If she'd care to come and hear him, he'd pick her up at four o'clock and get her home by midnight.

She let herself gush with regret, puffing O's with her full pale lips. "I'd love to hear you so much, Ed, but Roy is taking me to a lecture on 'The True Story of Oscar Wilde' at the opera house. So, you see."

27

"Who's he?"

"A great English writer. Mama heard him give a reading once *in person* when she was my age. She said he was so uplifting! She's positive he was slandered at that terrible trial. Such *little* people—they just can't stand to think someone near them's great. I remember Miss Flynn told us, and everybody said she was the best teacher Miss Turner's ever had: it seldom pays to pry into the private lives of great poets. Take Charles Lamb, such a dear man—he drank gin! There's always a bright side. The speaker Saturday writes, too, for a big New York newspaper."

"Going with Roy, huh. Well, have a good time."

But Thursday Roy called off their date. In the past couple of days, three children had died of diphtheria and five more had bad symptoms. She thought of five, square, dark-red signs nailed to five front doors: Q U A R A N T I N E in black letters. If Roy had been properly sad, her excitement would have made her feel closer to him; but no matter how hard he held onto the reins, he couldn't disguise little signs that betrayed how important he was feeling—secret smile, the way his eyes blinked, the way he slapped the back of one hand in the palm of the other—and she was seriously offended with him.

"Why in the name of Aunt Hannah did you turn in the tickets, Roy? I wanted to go. Don't you ever think of others?"

"But, precious, I *was* thinking of you. Diptheria is contagious."

"*Diph*theria."

"Have it your way. Anyhow, it's always wise to stay home when there's a threat of an epidemic."

"It's really and truly a genuine epidemic?"

"Doc Roos said not to use the word around, folks'd panic. But it is."

"Really?"

He nodded, right as usual.

"I'm sorry," she said with downcast eyes.

In fact she was not so much sorry as let down. Worse, she felt Roy was thinking to himself that she'd let him down.

She wanted to skip rehearsal that night. She was afraid that

28

Ed would give her a long-suffering, martyred look. At supper her father patted her hand and asked, "What's the matter with my little warbler?" She realized she had been babying herself. She caught up his hand and kissed it; she said she had been letting the thought of the quarantine prey on her mind, she'd quit being silly right now. She went up to her room without dessert and, sitting with her back to the mirror, brushed her hair for half an hour, humming softly. By the time she came back downstairs, she'd snapped out of it.

In fact, she was feeling so good that, as they were walking to church, she whistled right out loud on the public street, and when her mother, scandalized, tried to hush her, she tossed her head and kept on whistling. When she saw Ed leaning back against the pulpit, somber, alone, she made a mock-gloomy face at him, hid in her muffler, jerked it off, and openly gave him a full smile. He walked straight up to her.

"Roy tells me he's got funerals. I returned him a book to-night."

"It's terrible. Have you heard? We almost have an epidemic."

"Nobody's sick out our way that I've heard of."

"Dr. Roos says . . ."

"So you can come out to Foster's Saturday night? You said you'd like to if you could."

"Oh!" Why had she smiled at him at all? Where was some-one to rescue her? Mona was sidling up the aisle in their direc-tion. His eyes pleaded; his stern eyes begged her. "All right.— Oh, Mona, isn't it awful?"

Ed laid his hand on her forearm. "I'll call for you at four o'clock."

His crudeness—it was hard to deal with. And Mona's keen eyes! Muriel blushed and nodded. "We may be going to have a real epidemic. I've never been in quarantine, have you? The next few days will tell."

During rehearsal her mother had to keep nudging her to make her stand still.

She didn't mention Ed's invitation till noon next day at the dinner table. Her sister asked if she'd told Roy. "I haven't yet."

Her mother urged her to dance a lot and be sure to remember each little thing—"such a new experience." Her father began reminiscing about a hoedown in Virginia the year he'd gone East to visit his cousins on his mother's side.

"Fiddlers like that you never did hear, niggers. They'd just been slaves not too long ago. They kept time with a sort of a bounce in their knee. One of them was blowing in a jug somehow." He began thunking and making jug noises till they were screaming with laughter.

Her mother, in her special voice, said, "Eugene, we are at table," and everyone fell silent. Her father got up, without a word, his face blank, and went back to his office.

Muriel thought she oughtn't to disturb Roy with a silly little thing like a barn dance. What he was doing really was important, what with the diphtheria on top of everything else. She would run into him in a store or somewhere and mention the subject in passing without making a big issue of it. A barn dance, for heaven's sake—what's that? It turned out she had no call to so much as step out of the house all day Friday or Saturday before four; so there didn't turn out to be a chance to tell him. She just let the whole thing slide.

As Ed helped her into the buggy and tucked the blankets snug around her, she felt a pang lest Roy see them. It would be terribly embarrassing. She determined to speak out to Ed as soon as they got to the edge of town where they weren't apt to be interrupted, at the powerhouse, say. She didn't care who else saw her with Ed, just so long as they got out of town without running into Roy. The instant they reached the powerhouse, safe, she said, "I ought to let you know, Roy and I are going to be engaged soon."

"So they tell me."

"So who tells you?"

"Mona."

"But it's for me to tell people."

"Hey," he said, reining in the horse, "you've got tears in your eyes. Shoot, now, what is it?"

30

"I'm mad, that's all, I'm just plain mad."

"Well, she didn't hurt anything. You look pretty enough to me to let a crippled girl be as jealous of you as she feels like."

He'd told her that she was pretty. He wanted to make her feel good. She wiped her tears on his coat sleeve, smiled, and snuggled his arm.

He clucked. "She's a good horse, Dolly." They watched the dun haunches jounce. "Plowing, gathering corn, courting, she's good for what needs to be done slow but sure. Queenie's faster, but Dolly here knows what's needed."

She wasn't sure what he was talking about, but she was sure that it wasn't just horses. It was her duty to deflect him. "Tell me what missionary school was like. How long did you stay there?"

"Four months. It's what it ought to be." He sounded a bit surly; he stared straight ahead.

"Goodness, you're not sorry you went?"

He gave her a sidewise, yet haughty glance, and he licked his narrow lips. "No, I'm not. I learned something there that badly needed to be found out. What do you imagine I had in mind when I went?"

"To be a missionary. To save the souls of natives."

"Sure, that was it. As simple as that. That's all there was to it, save souls."

He took the whip handle and jabbed Dolly at the root of her tail. She snorted and began to trot.

"There was one professor—he was really just a preacher D.D., but they all got called professors—Harlan Shattuck, been in China, not a whole lot older than me, I'm twenty-eight— one day Harlan asked if we had the calling. No. I've got to keep what he said straight. I'm putting a sorry burden on him, to let one thing he said change my life. The least I can do is to be fair about what he said."

Ed was talking at Dolly's rump. He did not seem to be explaining himself so much as letting Muriel overhear his thoughts. She hardly breathed.

"Harlan asked if we knew how to tell whether we had a true calling. He began listing lots of things that can poison a true call-

31

ing without a person's noticing. Most of his list passed me by, but one didn't. He put it this way. Do you ever have a picture of yourself before an altar, in a robe, maybe a cross up there behind you, with your arms stretched out and hundreds of little dark people coming to be saved at your hands? The more he painted that picture the more I squirmed. I was that man. 'Ambition,' Harlan said, 'power.' I knew it. The picture showed me. A person may be saddled with ambition, but he ought to find better things to do with it than lording it over some unsuspecting heathens. So I left school."

"Did you tell them why?"

"Harlan. The others, I'd lost the calling. Which was the truth, too—one side of it, anyway, gussied up nice, the way truth usually is when it gets out in public. If you're saving other people's souls in order to make yourself feel good, you won't save many."

It would be a mistake for her to say anything to him after that. She snuggled closer.

His body yielded a little. "You're the funny one. Who'd have guessed I'd be telling you all that stuff?"

Roy had never made her feel this good. Roy knew right where he was going. Which was not far. Enough of that. She put Roy out of her mind.

Ed's three brothers seemed shy of her, but his married sister Fran was friendly. Babies—Fran was going to have her first in March, so they talked babies. Ed stayed near Muriel while they ate, but when the dancing started, he seemed somehow to lose track of her. He only danced twice, neither time paying her much notice. Of course, the dances were square or polka, schottische or round, everybody together, no real partners. Still.

Two or three times Ed disappeared with a friend among the dark stalls. She was sure they had a corn liquor jug there; when they first came in, she'd seen a white earthenware gallon jug in a manger; sweet cider came in brown ones. She noticed grimly that when he sauntered back in the lantern light, half-shrugging, fists jammed in pockets, he avoided catching her eye.

"That Ed, we call him the odd-Bell," said Fran. "He wasn't

32

but a kid when they had that war in China. He was keen on going. He said all he wanted to be was a drummer boy, but he was practicing shooting the twenty-two down in the swale. Dad had to take a razor strop to him to keep him to home. And yet, shucks, Ed can't hardly bear to slaughter a pig. He'll do it, but you'd think it was a murder, he frowns so when he sticks the knife in their necks."

The older man's calling was livelier than Ed's, better to dance to, but not for worlds would Muriel have told Ed anything but what a wonderful caller he was. And he *was* good; she was only slightly disappointed. The last dance, of course, was a waltz. Ed held her somewhat rigidly, but they kept good time together, and he bowed like a gentleman.

"I told Fran we'd drop her off home. I hope you don't mind? It's not more'n half a mile."

"Mind! I have no right to mind even if I wanted to, which I don't. Good heavens."

"I just thought I'd ask."

Ed helped his sister first into the two-wheeled buggy. "Move over, Fran, I want Muriel in the middle." He tucked the robe over the two women, and sat against Muriel, who squeezed his arm. When he bent near to say "All set?" their breaths blended in the dim air and wisped away together. All she smelled from him was tobacco, a manly smell. Flakes of light snow seemed not to be falling so much as rocking in the moonlight.

"Owen druv me in," said Fran, "but he wouldn't stay for misery. 'Land-o'-Goshen,' I said to him, 'Sweetie, I'm not fit to dance either, but I'm a-going anyhow.' Now, Muriel, I can swear by you I didn't dance a step, did I? You was with me nearly all night. Owen's left foot still bothers him from August, right up a little ways from the second toe where he speared a pitchfork through it haying. The tine was clean so he didn't get lockjaw, which is a blessing, for we hadn't been married but seven months, and thank the Lord it missed his bones. I just like the fiddling so much, and I'm crazy for calling. You keep it up, Ed, in a year you'll be as good as Bunkum Lorry."

"More'n a year, Fran." He winked past Muriel at her.

"Not better, as good. Mark my words. Well, anyway, you know Owen, he likes to dance as much as me. He's got it fixed some way in his noodle that it'd be bad on that sore if he stayed around the music. He'd have to hold back so darned hard to keep from kicking out and hopping around and jumping up and clicking his heels like he wants to that it'd cramp on the hole in his foot. That's what he thinks anyways. So I said to him, 'Just take me, I can always get a ride home.' So I can swear by you, can't I, Muriel?"

When they were nearly up the lane, a lantern swung out in the yard.

"Owen!" she yelled. "Sweetie pie! Where's your coat?"

He swung her down. "Your nose is cold, hon. Ed, I thank you for bringing my little girl home safe and sound."

"Shoot, now," Fran said. "Muriel, I'd like you to meet my hubby. Owen, this is Muriel Storr, Doc Storr's girl." They were pleased to meet. "Now, listen to me, O. I swear to high heaven I didn't dance one single time."

Muriel assured him she didn't. He stood behind Fran and pulled her up against him, his hands hammocking her belly, heisting it up a little. Muriel thought it terribly uncouth of him to call attention to her protruding abdomen this way, but Fran didn't seem to mind, just rubbing her head in against the side of his neck.

"J. Q. Morley's got him a machine, Ed. He druv by to see if we could sing for the Odd Fellows next Friday."

"It's fine with me."

"Same with Dick and Mort. So it's all set. Stanley Cross's going to be investitured."

"That a fact?"

As they drove away, Muriel tucked the robe over Ed's legs and said the proper thing: "My, such warm, friendly people." But she was thinking: There's nothing the matter with him that keeping him away from his family won't cure; when he's given a chance, he'll just rise of his own accord. "Are you still working on your father's farm?"

34

"My brothers are big enough now to take over. I've been working on it since I was knee-high to a grasshopper." He glanced at her shyly. "That's your Dad's expression, I know, but I hope he won't mind if I help myself to it."

She hugged his arm. "I don't mind either."

For a mile he said nothing. The snow had stopped. His breathing was heavy. She watched Dolly plod. The reins went slack. He tried to rear his arm around her, but their coats made it too clumsy. His gloved hand pressed her mittened hand steadily and very hard. He was neither in a fumbling rush nor tentative.

Ahead of time, Muriel liked having boys wanting to kiss her; and, afterward, she liked even more having been kissed. But the kissing itself, at the time . . . Still, she did not mind it too much, if it wasn't too *special*. Sometimes a kiss of Roy's would linger in her mind against her will. They would start out casually, just fine; by the time their kisses began to soften and lengthen and reach, she could not resist, she could barely remember she was supposed to want to resist. Afterward, though, she would resent him as much as she'd loved it at the time. Having been kissed by Roy was no longer anything special; yet the way he did it was very special; yet it was special in a way she could not tell anybody else about because she didn't know what to make of it. She tried to keep it a secret even from herself, but that was too much for her. So she resented him.

Ed kissed her on the cheek. She sat like a lump, her cheek feeling hardly anything, it was so cold. There started to grow up in her mind the picture of Roy putting wax doodads shaped like halves of apples inside the cheeks of a corpse to round them out; he'd described it once before she made him quit telling about *that*. Before that picture got too vivid, Ed, without trying to snuggle, turned her face with his free hand and pressed his cold lips against hers, at the same time breathing as hard as Roy would breathe after five long kisses. She felt his stubble scrape her chin. His cold stiff lips did not unfold but pressed hard against her mouth; too hard; it hurt a little. She was not softening against her better judgment, not losing her self-possession. Like a holy wafer,

35

his saltless kiss came to her lips, no flavor, a mystery, all a signature.

"Muriel, I wish you'd wait for me."

"Gracious, are you going away?"

"I would ask you to marry me if only I had a living."

"But I told you that Roy and I . . . You know, we're . . . New Year's Day. We planned to tell and . . ."

"Roy's a good man, but here you are. Muriel, I promise to ask you by next September. Will you wait?"

"Oh," she said, "that's such a long time. Besides, why don't you ask me now?"

"I'd rather fix it up this way."

Dolly had quit walking. Her tail arched and switched. Globes of turds welled out steaming and plopped on the gravel right in front of them. Ed seemed to take no notice. Muriel considered asking him to move on; but then, it might be rude to interrupt his flow of thoughts; besides, he was a farmer. And too, somehow, like this, the odor seemed pleasant (she could never in this world have said so out loud, *really* it was unpleasant).

"September?" she said. "I can't see why."

"There shouldn't be much of a lapse between a woman saying 'I will' to her man and 'I do' in front of a preacher. I've noticed there's nothing 'I will' gives birth to faster than 'I won't,' at least in one half of the human race. If you wait for me I'll come back."

"But you'll come by and see me, won't you?"

"Some."

"I mean, we have to talk about things."

"Sure."

"Well, what do you mean, 'come back'?"

"Ties. I mean I'm free till then to look around for what I want to do. Till I come back and ask you for real, and you take me, we'll both of us be free. No ties." They looked into one another silently. Dolly champed and stomped. "Whoa, girl, hold steady."

This time when they kissed, she felt him trembling. "All

36

right, Ed, I'll wait." He looked as though he might cry. She laid her head on his shoulder. "Oh, dear, what shall I say to Roy?"

"The truth, I guess." He shook the reins. "You'd better tell him you don't love him."

2

Young Wife

The farm they sharecropped from Muriel's mother's sweet old maid first cousin twice removed, Hypatia Gunn, lay southeast between Dunreith and Bettancourt. The previous tenant broke his neck falling in the empty silo when a rotten ladder rung gave. Ed paid his widow, Mrs. Watkins, a good price for the team of mules, and she went back home to Iowa with her two boys; all they took with them fit in two suitcases, an old trunk, and an apple crate. After Hypatia took her half of what Ed harvested that fall, she took most of the other half for what Watkins had owed her; she explained to Ed that this was fair because she was letting him use the farm equipment free and also because he and Muriel got all the Watkins furniture. "All!" cried Muriel when he told her this. "All these pitiful little scraps of junk!" By Christmastime the Storrs saw to it that the house was set up properly ("for our little girl"), and Muriel had stowed every single thing the Watkinses had left away in the spare bedroom or up in the attic.

Ed's silly sister Ethel had given them a carom set for a wedding present. Muriel insisted Ed and she play caroms sometimes. He grumbled that it was a fool children's game, but she'd bring out the board once a week or so, reminding him it was dear Ethel who gave it to them. He could flip the wooden rings five times harder than she could, and he always won. He was better than she was at checkers, at 500, at double solitaire—even at her favorite game cooncan, which he wanted to call rummy but she wouldn't let him, cooncan was so colorful, so *frontiersy*, as her mother put it. Well, she would just let him beat her at games all he liked; she would conserve her energy for bigger issues such as his singing.

The first few weeks, they attended the Bells' church, the Calvary Baptist Church of Dunreith. But Muriel told Ed she didn't feel right, somehow, without more ceremony. These Baptists took communion, which they called the Lord's Supper, only at Easter, and what they called wine was thimblefuls of sweet grape juice on a tray which the ushers passed down from the aisles; the preacher wore a suit and tie, and not even the choir wore robes; even at Christmas they thought it was daring to have altar candles, and it would never occur to them to have incense; they said *Gawd*. Ed went with her to one service at Trinity, then balked —men wearing lace, people kneeling in public. She was willing to move halfway to meet him, to the Methodists (they had at least descended from the Church of England), but they were too far from Calvin for Ed to feel easy about it. In Bettancourt there was a Presbyterian Church which they agreed to try.

She found *some* familiar ceremony. She had anticipated bellows of hellfire and brimstone; instead, Dr. Everson's hour-long sermon pounded away on how to interpret signs that God was glad with a soul. The main sign was success; the message the congregation was left with was, you must exercise your will because get-up-and-go was the way to make a success of yourself; the text was, "There but for the grace of God go I," because after all success didn't mean anything in itself, but only as a sign of grace, which God grants as it suits Himself not us. All her life, Muriel had been hearing how fine success was; still, she almost closed her ears, she felt so risky hearing it said from a pulpit; still, maybe success was not *just* a business matter, maybe it could be spiritual as well. Dr. Everson was a splendid preacher, no doubt of that, and he pronounced *God* the way it ought to be. In the cold buckboard riding home, Ed complained that Dr. Everson had gone on too long and that, after church on the front steps, he had urged them too hard to come to Wednesday prayer meeting. She eagerly agreed. She hoped Ed would bring up success so she could let him know what was bothering her; he didn't mention it; she didn't want to bring it up first.

She had grown up hearing plainsong chanted in the high, old manner by a choir of men and boys. "Didn't the hymns just hurt your ears?"

To Ed, hymn-singing was a way of shouting unto the Lord. "Well, they felt strange to me."

"I'm so glad you agree with me! Weren't they ugly?"

"Ugly," he repeated in a troubled voice, but he didn't go on. "I guess we'd might as well go back to Dunreith to the folks' church."

Surrounded by the whole Bell clan, with worse hymns yet! "Oh, honey, can't we please just try the Methodist Church one more time? I'm sure we'll learn to feel at home."

"We live too near Dunreith. The folks'll hold it ill in us to snoot them."

"Do we have to, Ed?"

"Yes, we ought."

Well, she'd put a good face on it. "You won't mind if I observe Lent and take communion on Easter? And maybe go on Christmas Eve? The candlelight service is *so* lovely at Trinity."

"All right." Then he burst out with a snatch of hymn, " 'Oh, holy Three in One,' " and they both gave way to laughter. Muriel, though, was scandalized as she always was when he sang this phrase; it seemed almost blasphemous of him; the first time he had done it he had been oiling her sewing machine and the brand name on the little can of oil was Three-in-One.

After she had washed the dishes and he had bedded down the

40

stock, they sat by the Franklin stove in the living room, and he read aloud in a solemn voice the passage from *Paradise Lost* of Adam and Eve offering fruit to an angel, fearing nothing, naked, unashamed. At nine, she lighted the candle, turned down the coal oil lamp, and was standing hand cupped beyond the chimney to blow the flame out, when Ed said, "I don't want to go back to the folks' church in Dunreith any more than you do, dear. In a new county we could join the Methodists easy enough. If we set aside some money, pretty soon we'll be able to move someplace where it'd be easier on both of us."

She sat on his lap and hugged him, eyes brimming with gratitude for his thoughtfulness. They kissed longer than they had kissed before. His flat lips never softened the way Roy's had done; they never moved on their own; she had to press back equally hard or else—he didn't know his own strength—he would crush her lips against her teeth; once, her lower lip had bled. This time, however, she did not resist him for her own protection, but felt herself everywhere strenuously "rising to the occasion," in her mother's expression; she joined him in the kiss.

She put off getting into bed; she could feel him in there waiting. It was cold. She was breathing oddly, a puff, then nothing, puff nothing, puff nothing. When she got in, he hugged her, hard. On these occasions, she had always lain like a lump, nervous and rigid at once, stabbed with peculiar sensations. Tonight, suffused with what he'd said and with that new kiss, she could not help moving to his touch. She tried to follow what went on among the odors from the dark pouring from under the blankets after he pulled up her nightgown. She could not. The ferocious stab scattered her thoughts every which way. The midnight before their wedding, her sister had said she'd never paid any attention to what her husband had done *down there*, just let him do it; you have to. But Muriel's feelings now were so strong her head could not keep out the pleasure that burst deep inside her abdomen. The lovely threat was swelling up toward her head and she had no words handy with which to keep it down in its place. Before it engulfed her, she fled into sleep.

Over the months, people began talking about that war in Europe as worse and worse, different from other wars; they called it The Great War. What Ed brought home was anecdotes of thieves falling out over loot, of godless, perfidious politicians. In Wichita, Muriel had got to know a German girl who was so nice; all the same, she felt sure England would win. She neither doubted nor believed that hundreds of thousands of men were living in open trenches trying to kill each other, but she knew for sure their feet must get cold. Whenever she could spare the time, she knitted socks, which the Red Cross said soldiers on both sides needed.

Meanwhile, the price of hogs began to rise. Ed planted as much of the farm as he could in corn, even ploughing under the field of clover, and pastured the two Guernsey cows in the apple orchard. Then, he built a pigpen, with a run down to the creek for their wallow, and went into debt to Hypatia enough more to buy two brood sows. He sang with the quartette as often as they could drum up invitations, and twice he was paid for soloing. The Old Soldiers Home invited him to sing on Memorial Day for nothing, but Muriel talked him into agreeing not to sing anywhere without at least some payment; he said all right but just this once he'd sing at the Home for nothing. She scrimped every way she could. He would just laugh when she mentioned that they could afford for him to take singing lessons, it would pay off in the end. She did not drop that plan; that was what she was *really* saving for. By their second anniversary they had nearly pulled out of debt, and the prices of corn and pork were still on the way up.

That Good Friday, war was declared. The next Monday the single member of the quartette joined the army. A week after, Muriel's brother Dick—he wasn't even eighteen—ran off to Wichita against his parents' wishes and enlisted. Muriel was so sure her mother would be needing her moral support that, since she had to go to town anyway to see Dr. Roos, she went home to stay the night, as she did occasionally. Dr. Roos confirmed her suspicion. She was going to have a baby. At least he thought it more than likely. Her mother heeded her announcement little

42

more than if she was a church friend—"Isn't it wonderful"—and when she talked to Muriel about Dick she was obviously just "putting a good face on things." That night her parents went up to their bedroom right after supper, and she heard their voices surge and sink till all hours. In her childhood bed, Muriel cried herself to sleep. She woke up sometime in the night; it was silent and dark; before she realized where she was, her hand reached out to take hold of Ed as she did when she had a bad dream; it butted the wall.

Next morning she walked the miles to her own home, ashamed of herself: her husband should have been the first to hear her news, she was a married woman now. The ground was beginning to thaw, but the sun was still too thin to take the edge off the breeze. She built a good fire in the kitchen stove, though it was early to start dinner, huddled over it shivering, and had to fight her tears back. What was wrong with her? There was nothing in this world she had ever wanted more than a baby. Maybe it was just changes in the body chemistry. Dr. Roos had warned her she might get emotional sometimes.

Huddling, she determined she would begin to knit as soon as the shivers stopped. But though they stopped after a while, somehow she couldn't bring herself to start knitting but just crouched on a stool by the stove nibbling hangnails. Then the snort of a mule and the clatter of the wagon and Ed's singing *Whoa, boys!* shook her out of her spell, and she ran out into the yard eager to tell him. But he showed her with dancing eyes the new brood sow, still a gilt, he had in the wagon in a crate; he'd paid as much for her as for both the others, and he spoke of corn, of planting the whole farm in corn, even the kitchen patch in corn, nothing but corn and hogs: money.

Thrumming with his excitement, she went back in and cooked—pink beans with bacon rind, cole slaw, and today, as a special treat for him, apple pie. One of the first things she'd done as soon as they were married was to cut down, drastically, on pies because of his sick headaches. He'd grumped, but she knew best: he'd only had one sick headache in months. He'd never been to a dentist once and was mortally scared to go to one, but

43

she had got him to promise he would go to her father when he "could find the time."

Corn and hogs. She already knew how she missed looking out the window above the sink onto the green pasture, how she missed the smell of clover, nature's incense, and how much she hated the stench of hogs. Ed's confidence of profit reconciled her to rows of tall corn. As they ate she begged him to keep the hen-house and the fenced garden patch; she'd look after them; having their own fresh eggs and vegetables meant so much to her. He squeezed her hand, winked, and said of course he'd help her. He praised her for the pie, and said today was a new beginning.

"Ed, I'm going to have a baby."

She collapsed in hot tears, somehow fearful to go bury her face in his bosom as she felt like. He came around the table and gathered her in his arms. He held her for a long time, saying that their cup was running over.

When he went back out to work, she stood at the screen door and watched him walk across the yard, and she could feel proud love fill her heart, driving the silliness from it. "How Firm a Foundation" sang itself in her ears. All afternoon she kept thinking about their very own place which Ed swore "by all that's holy" they would own before their child was ready to go to school.

The next day—the very next day as Muriel said over and over to Ed afterward, never daring to utter the big word that kept rising in her mind, *providential*—the next day Hypatia Gunn had a total stroke. Ed found her. He'd gone over to her house first thing after breakfast to tell her about the bred gilt; she'd advanced the cash for it. He was also, at Muriel's instigation, going to begin softening her up to do better than the present fifty-fifty terms he was sharecropping on; he was the best tenant she'd ever had, and she'd do better forty-sixty with him than fifty-fifty with anybody else. She didn't answer his knock. Where could she be at eight in the morning? She wasn't out feeding the poultry. Something must be wrong. Two years earlier she'd had a partial stroke, which she'd recovered from. He

44

didn't hesitate more than a second to pry open the cellar door. He went up into the house, calling her name. He told Muriel that, when he first saw Hypatia on her side in the upstairs hall-way, he thought she was dead, he couldn't see signs of breathing, but then he rolled her on her back and saw her eyes.

"It's funny. Her face was just like a corpse, and her eyes didn't move. But I swear she was looking at me. I could feel her doing it. I just knew she was alive."

"Did you see anything in her eyes? Fear?"

"No, not fear, nothing remotely like it. Nor confusion either, the way old people get. She knew. She was still in charge. The same old Hypatia. You know what I fancy? I fancy she was watching me to make sure I took care of her right."

"Bossy."

"All right, but you've got to hand it to her. She's a great old bird."

"Mean old commander bird."

"Have it your way."

"It's so sad to think she hasn't got any family to stand by her."

"Well, your mother's with her this very minute."

"Yes, but I mean children, brothers and sisters. Oh, what a mercy it would be if she would only go quickly."

Hypatia died during the night.

Muriel kept telling Ed and her mother how merciful Hypatia's passing had been. Her mother agreed wholeheartedly, and Ed grunted a time or two more or less in agreement.

The afternoon after the funeral, the will was read in Hypatia's house. It turned out, to everyone's surprise, that Hypatia had bequeathed to Muriel the farm that she and Ed were living on.

It hadn't even occurred to Muriel to go to the reading of the will, and Ed was out mending fence when her mother came by with the news. Eighty acres! Their own home! A well-stocked farm! "That Hypatia, she drives a hard bargain"—that's what people had always said. But what kind of a bargain was this bequest? Muriel had just been nice to her when she was obliged to. *Providential* swelled in Muriel's mind unspeakably; *merciful* and

45

thankful got so noisy in her mouth that her mother had to give her an SLH (a Subtle Little Hint). When Ed came in and heard about it, he offered up a prayer of thanksgiving right there in the front room. Oh, he was so good, and his faith was so strong.

After supper, the two of them sat at the kitchen table drinking hot cocoa—their special Sunday treat.

"The Lord has seen fit to favor us," said Ed, "and the least we can do is to make the best of what He has bestowed upon us."

"Of course, honey, and that's why we must be so careful to make sure what the best thing for us to do is."

"When you've got a farm, farm it. A farm tells you what to do."

"Yes, but I can't help thinking about the parable where the master is going on a long trip and he leaves talents with the three servants and one of them doesn't do anything with his but hide it away out of harm's way while the others did something with what they had so it multiplied. 'The single talent well-employed,' something, something, 'which it is death to hide.' "

"Oh, now, Muriel, in the Bible a talent means a sum of money, and what we've got is a farm."

"Which can be turned into money."

"Money! Turn God's land into money? Not till we have to."

"Now, honey," she said, "look, we didn't get the farm from God exactly, we got it from Hypatia."

"You got it from Hypatia."

"All right, *I* got it. But what *you* got from God, directly, is a real, genuine, honest-to-goodness talent. A voice. You can sing."

"Well, yes, I know," he said, "but . . ."

"We've got to discuss it, honey, that's all there is to it. Seriously."

"All right, but one thing I know is," he said hitting the table with the flat of his hand, "a farm's a farm."

It seemed unwise to her, under the circumstances, to pursue the subject any further tonight. "Of course, sweetie, of course. I just thought we ought to discuss it, that's all."

They discussed it every night for two weeks. By then, they were pretty well agreed that, as between farming and singing, his

46

chances of success were safer with farming but much much grander with singing. He feared he was too old, but she said it was never too late to try. She wanted him to go to the best man in Chicago, or at least St. Louis; but he put his foot down.

"Kansas City is big city enough for me. It's going to cost a fortune any way you look at it, and there's good enough voice teachers in Kansas City to tell me whether it's worth my time going on."

She thought this was probably true. "All right, Ed, I'm sure you know what's best. But if he does say yes—and I don't have the slightest doubt in the world he will—we've got to keep New York in mind. That's where the really great teachers are."

"The East." He opened the back door and spat out into the yard. "The East."

From the heavy scowl that curdled his face and from the way he stomped up to bed without even saying good night (the first time!), she saw this topic was even more delicate than she had realized; it would be needing a great deal more discussion in the future.

Sven Larsson gave them the name of his teacher in Kansas City—"the best man west of the Mississippi." Ed wrote and got an appointment early in June.

Late in the morning of the day Ed left, Hypatia's next-of-kin, a nephew from Tulsa, showed up unannounced. First he went to the lawyer, then to Muriel. He told her that since Hypatia had only loaned the farm equipment Ed would have to pay for it or give it back. Muriel's mother had scarcely heard of this squinchy-eyed nephew before, and the price he set for Ed to pay was outrageous. He even claimed the team of mules was Hypatia's, and of course they didn't have any written proof that they had paid Mrs. Watkins for them. No one even knew her address for sure anymore.

The second day Ed was gone, Muriel lost her baby. Thank the stars, she was home with her mother at the time. "The Lord giveth," her father said, "and the Lord taketh away." Which was true, but she couldn't help thinking that if that evil, ugly, conniving nephew hadn't come along at exactly the worst time it

47

would never have happened. Dr. Roos told her there was nothing to be alarmed about and not to pamper herself.

The third evening Ed returned, with bad news. The voice coach had told him he had a fine voice, no doubt of that, but it would take him months or even years just to breathe right, much less all the other things he had to learn; it would probably be a waste of money for him to go on with serious training.

Muriel felt her whole life collapsing. The final touch was Ed's reaction. If he'd looked happy, or even relieved, when he told her the coach's verdict, she could not have stood it, she would have just died. Not, of course, that he looked that way; but he didn't look miserable either. He looked grave and steady, the same as when she told him about losing the baby. The news about Hypatia's nephew seemed to bother him the most. But then, she'd often noticed Ed was too much in awe of lawsuits, money, businessmen. Still, he was a good man—a very good man. She'd have to pick up the pieces of her life and go on.

She begged him desperately—*some*thing had to be put right—to go to her father and have his teeth fixed. Patting her arm soberly, he said he would make an appointment the very next day when he drove into town for feed.

She began to put on weight.

Sunday after church, Ed's father wanted them to come spend the afternoon, but Muriel whispered to Ed that she just had to be home alone with him. He told them he had a lot of work to do to make up for the three days he'd lost going to Kansas City. When he said that, when he took the burden onto himself so generously, even though it was a little burden, she loved him more than she had since he'd got back.

While she started dinner, he went to the barn, still in his Sunday clothes, to check things over. In a short time she saw him returning, mud on his shoes and pants legs, holding something to his bosom with both hands, scowling. She held the screen door open for him and peeked inside his hands. It was a piglet.

"That sow," he said, "that devil-sow, she farrowed while we were at church and ate her litter."

48

"Oh no!" she cried, and her hands clapped over her ears. "How do you know? Are you sure?"

"I saw her finish one off. This one got under a rail somehow, but she'd have rooted it out before long."

"Ed Ed Ed." Her breath came in gasps. "It's so horrible. Maybe there are more coming."

"Maybe. Here." He held the pig out to her. Despite the heavy anger of his disappointment, he was gentle with the tiny creature. It looked naked and raw. She didn't want to touch it, but it looked so pitiful, so helpless, when he held it out to her cradled in his big callused hands. "I've got to change into my work clothes and go out and stay with her till I'm sure. The she-devil. Do you realize how much money we've thrown away on her? Sometimes sows eat a few of their young, but this is the first one I ever saw that ate them all. A prize she is. Precious bacon she'll make."

The piglet squealed just as Muriel lifted it into her hands.

"The poor little orphan," she said. "So pink." It felt warm and active, firm of flesh, squirmy. "Pinky's your name, baby." She kissed its tiny snout. "I just happen to have a bottle with a rubber nipple here in the cupboard, Pinky, and lots and lots of good cow's milk. How would you like that? Pinky? Pinky?"

By the time Ed got back to the barn, the sow had thrown another and was eating it. He stayed for two more hours, watching, but she was through.

"By God," he said when he finally came in, "that's one hog I won't mind slaughtering."

"Ed! Such language!"

She kept Pinky on her lap as they were eating. She'd made a vinegar pie for Ed, one of his favorites. She didn't allow herself to have hurt feelings when he didn't even comment on the pie and only ate half a piece.

Prices boomed. It was the worst war in all history. We were winning of course. Uncle Sam needed farmers, so Ed was safe from the draft. Her brother wrote that he'd had a miraculous battlefield escape, though his hearing was impaired at least temporar-

49

ily; but his closest buddy was in the hospital shell-shocked. What did *shell shock* mean, really? Nobody could answer that question to her satisfaction. It was always pressed in on her mind like cold pressing on a warm house in winter—*shell shock, shell shock.* She knitted many many socks. People kept assuring each other that, now America was in it, the war would be drawing to a rapid close. She wished she had known at least one evil German in her life so she could begin to understand how Germany could commit all those atrocities.

At first she was afraid to leave Pinky alone at night, but Ed put his foot down: the pig was to sleep on the back porch and was not to be allowed anywhere in the house but the kitchen, ever. Of course Ed was right, but the first night she went down to Pinky's box three or four times, replenishing the hot water bottle, feeding and hugging the little creature, just to make sure.

Pinky turned out to be a he, but by the time Muriel realized this the name was so much a part of him she could not bear to change it. When people commented on it, she smiled enigmatically.

He followed her everywhere. By the time he was six weeks old, he had a special pick-me-up squeal for her. He was brown with a black band around his middle and one black eye. He loved clabber, and Ed set up a keg for clabber by the back steps where she could dish out a panful for her piggy whenever she felt like it. At three months Ed said he'd never seen a finer shoat in his life, it was a sin and a shame about that devil of a mother of his. Muriel bent down and hugged him, making little throat noises.

"But, Mama!" she cried to herself. "He's so clean, really. Pigs don't have a chance out there in the mud. It just brings out the worst in them and they wallow. They *like* to wallow. But Pinky's as clean and neat as a cat. Of course I haven't exactly got him housebroken yet, but you can't expect everything."

"Muriel!"

"I just love him so."

"Mur-i-el!"

"I do, so there."

50

Ed decided to pay Hypatia's nephew what he was asking. "I could find as good equipment for less money, but it would be trouble locating it." Of course he refused to pay again for the mules, no matter what. "Anyhow, it's not like we didn't get the farm for nothing. Oh, I know he isn't the one we owe anything to, but still." The real reason, to Muriel's mind that Ed was going to pay was to avoid a lawsuit or even talking to a lawyer any more than he could help. But she didn't confront him with her suspicion. It was a weakness in him, no doubt of that. He might have thought she didn't have respect for him, though of course she did.

Instead, when he talked about taking out more of a mortgage than necessary to pay for the equipment, so as to build up the farm and livestock, especially to buy more brood sows, she put up every argument she could think of, short of tears, trying to dissuade him. He got that stubborn *Bell* look around his mouth and borrowed the money anyway. She acted as though she cared a lot, though as a matter of fact she was secretly pleased at his determination. Maybe he was leery of lawyers, but that didn't mean he couldn't be a success in life.

She began to get letters from Rosemary Stonehouse, now McPherson, who was living in a town with the exotic name of Santa Rosa. Preston was doing even better than his uncle had promised he would, and the climate was just about perfect. Muriel loved exchanging letters with Rosemary. They found they had even more in common than they had realized. For one thing, Rosemary was so much wittier in her letters than she ever had been in conversation, and of course this stimulated Muriel to be at *her* best in their correspondence. She couldn't match Rosemary's wit, but she was good at making interesting little stories out of things that occurred.

She couldn't get used to the Bells—so uncouth. Of course it would be disloyal to Ed to mention this to anybody, even her mother. Especially her mother, who would pick up any SLH she might happen to let slip. For example, when she told her about one of Mother Bell's Sunday dinners, how much grease there was

51

in the flour gravy, she paused just for a second and gave one blink of her eyelids. She did not raise her voice or her eyebrows in any way, but she saw a twinkle of recognition in her mother's eyes. They would *never* talk openly about such a thing. With Rosemary, though—she was so far away—Muriel could let herself go and dress up a story to advantage, making it perfectly clear that she understood how people of Ed's folks' limited background would not have any understanding of diet and nutrition. She could not educate the whole Bell clan, but it was her duty as a wife to wean Ed off flour gravy and vinegar pies forever; she had started the process, but there was still a long way to go.

Rosemary had met only a few of the Ames people, so Muriel could give free rein to her descriptive powers. Roy and Mona had both pretty much dropped out of her life, for Ed and she naturally preferred seeing other young married couples. When she heard, through three or four different avenues, all very reliable, that Roy and Mona were seeing a lot of each other and were going to announce their engagement, she was officially delighted; but, in her letter to Rosemary about them, she got a treat out of going on about how *beautifully* matched those two were. A phrase occurred to her that seemed terribly witty, "an Odd Fellow undertaker and a crippled Unitarian," but by the time she had got the first half of it written down she realized the second half was too wicked to say even to Rosemary who didn't know them. Ashamed of herself, she changed it: "an Odd Fellow undertaker who is anything but odd, and Mona has such a lively interest in so many things in spite of her handicap."

She was rather cautious, at first, about mentioning Pinky to Rosemary. What she did was to take a stunt Pinky had performed one day and garnish it up till it made a cute little story. Rosemary's reaction was so wholeheartedly appreciative that from then on Muriel told her every little thing about him.

Really it wasn't about him so much as about the way people treated him; or no, more about the way they treated her for making a pet of him. She occasionally visited Naomi Arrowsmith, her nearest neighbor to the west, down the back road the better part of a mile; Naomi had darling two-and-a-half-year-old twin girls,

52

a little slow in some respects, but such sweet natures. Muriel took Pinky along when she dropped in on Naomi one morning. Of course he got awfully tired walking so far and she had to carry him partway, though he was getting too heavy. Naomi just couldn't get over the whole thing. "A pig, Muriel. Muriel, a pig!" The way she went on, you'd have thought it was the most interesting thing that had ever happened to her. Maybe it was, poor thing.

It got to be so that Muriel would begin to think of cute little things to do with Pinky. She said she did them just to see how people would react when she told about them, and that was true enough—it was *fun* to scandalize a D.A.R. function. But the main reason she did them was to have stories to tell Rosemary in her letters. Ed was the thorn in her flesh. He not only wouldn't allow Pinky in the house anymore, even in the kitchen; he began talking about slaughtering him. Her own wonderful Pinky! Of course she knew he was getting too big altogether; something would have to be done about him sometime; she would leave it up to Ed to decide what to do and when. But did Ed have to be so gruff about it? One Saturday afternoon they were going to drive in to Ames, and Muriel got Pinky all fixed up with a collar and a sort of leash made of ribbons of three different colors. He didn't really need a leash; he was so devoted to her he would follow her like Mary's little lamb. But she would make a concession because he had never been to town before, and maybe there would be dogs to upset him. But Ed, when she came with Pinky out to the buckboard, absolutely forbade her to take "the shoat" along. Did he have to be *so* callous about her feelings? She tried to talk the whole thing over on the ride in, but Ed's replies were just snorts. She had to think it over by herself. Of course he was right; it had been a silly idea of hers; Pinky would have been terrified. Who knows what might have happened to him in his alarm? And the town dogs! She wrote up the whole story for Rosemary with gusto, and only had to tell the whitest of white lies, about how *reasonable* Ed had been with her in her silliness, explaining *patiently* why he had to say no. It was one of her mother's cherished principles that a woman should always present

53

her husband in the most favorable light possible, and Muriel subscribed to this principle wholeheartedly. Besides, Rosemary knew how to read between the lines; Muriel wrote that, on the outskirts of Ames when they were beginning to run into passers-by, she dabbed at her eyes and put on her bravest smile; she was positive that Rosemary would know what she really meant.

"The saga of Pinky has come to its pathetic end." That is how she began her letter to Rosemary telling about Pinky's unfortunate demise. He had learned about the clabber keg. One day she forgot and left the lid off. He got on the top step and leaned in to guzzle all the clabber he could, but he lost his balance and fell in head first. Ed was the one to find him, on his way in to dinner. She put in her letter both the look of tenderness on Ed's face when he was consoling her and the sour look when he said it was too bad he hadn't found the pig in time to bleed him so he wouldn't go to waste. She'd stopped crying, but when he said this, she started in all over again. She had to get back at him for his callousness, his downright unkindness. She told Rosemary everything in this letter, even this about Ed. But she tried not to sound vindictive. "I have one consolation anyhow. Maybe Pinky died of his own unrestrained appetite, but at least no one got to eat him."

The war was going well for the allies, and that made her feel good too, even though it was such a horrible war. No one ever succeeded in making clear to her what it was all about. At first she thought this was because she was a silly goose of a woman, but then she began to suspect the men didn't know either and she quit asking. She left all the other political issues up to the men; she might as well leave the war too. Nothing excited her less than woman's suffrage.

Everything went well on the farm, and the price of hogs kept climbing steadily, "in spite of the middleman," Ed said. Uncle Sam needed farmers, and Ed was certainly doing all he could for his country. She was happy; by the end of the next summer, they were not only out of debt, they had a respectable beginning on a savings account.

Ed kept talking about buying machinery when they had enough saved up, but she had another plan. Of course she couldn't mention it while the war was still on; it didn't seem right to do anything that wouldn't help our boys over there, and she couldn't deny that her plan was selfish, just for their own personal benefit. They had to move. What a pity it was that Hypatia's farm had been so close to Dunreith. They had to move to another county. Of course that would mean she would be farther from her family, too, and she would miss her mother badly. All the same, for everybody's good, they had to do it—not too far away, though. She resolved to wait till the war was over; *then* she wouldn't rest until they had found another farm.

She began collecting reasons to move, for example, complaints Ed made from time to time about their present farm, to use as ammunition in case he opposed her. She wasn't much afraid he would, but, as her grandmother used to say, "Men are the strangest beings in the whole of God's creation." She would have to be prepared to get around him, in case.

Her real reason for wanting to move she couldn't mention to anybody: she felt sure that, once they were living in a new place, she would quit holding it against him that he had given up his career as a singer. She managed to keep from saying anything to anybody about these feelings, but bad thoughts about him kept coming into her mind, regardless. Sometimes, thinking ahead to when the war should be over—please, God, soon—she actually hoped that Ed would oppose the idea of moving. That way, their little difference of opinion would be out in the open, and she could just inkle to him *why*. By giving way to her, as he surely would then do, he would prove he truly loved her, and everything would be all right. Her mother's mother had come out to Kansas as a bride, when there were Indians and wolves to contend with, and Muriel told herself some of the pioneer spirit was still coursing through her veins.

But things turned out differently from what she had expected—as they so often did. The week before the Armistice, her father died of a heart attack. Between patients, without previous warning, he just fell to the floor and his heart never beat

55

again. It was a mercy, of course, to go like that if you had to go at all. But what was her mother to do with herself? And money —maybe she would have to live with her children. She was of an age at which she ought to remain near old friends, to say nothing of relatives. It would only make things worse for them to move away now.

It was Ed, in fact, who first mentioned moving. But he was not wholehearted about it, because the farm was doing so well it didn't seem sensible to leave. Besides, it was March when he brought the subject up, and the winter had been as cold and windy as anybody could remember; in weather like this, it was only natural for a person to think about a change. She was pretty sure that, once spring came, the subject wouldn't come up again for a long time. Ed loved flowers, and often, in season, he would bring in wild flowers, holding them gently in his big, hardened fingers, for her to arrange in a vase.

By May, not only was the weather gorgeous, but she knew she was pregnant again. So there was no question of moving, and they were happy. She decided to settle for switching to the Methodist Church, no matter what. That would be something of a move, and at the same time it would let her sing *some* good music. Sunday hymns were all the singing they still did, except around the house when they were feeling good or at a get-together at somebody's home.

That August, Ed fell off the hay wagon and broke his right leg, "a compound fracture," Dr. Roos called it, and he put Ed in a cast. Her brother Dick was home from the war by then, terribly changed. Moody; deaf in one ear and using his deafness to suit his own convenience; given to making bitter remarks; buttoned up about his experiences in France. He was just lounging around at home letting Mama take care of him, doing nothing much more than mowing the lawn and keeping the vegetable garden weeded. Muriel had even heard rumors he hung around the pool hall at night, and Mama certainly said he often didn't get up in the mornings till a disgraceful hour, ten, eleven, noon. So, it was all for the good that he had to come out to the farm and take over while Ed was laid up. He didn't want to but he did. After all, Ed and she were contributing something to help Mama out. Dick couldn't just live off other people all his life; he had to assume a man's responsibilities, even if he might have been shell-shocked. And besides, how could they know what that meant when he wouldn't discuss the subject? Shell-shocked.

He did the chores satisfactorily, Ed told her, and he kept regular hours, up early and early down. But he didn't like hogs. That was all right; they were hard to like. Ed sort of liked some of them and found nice things to tell her about them, and Muriel always reminded herself of Pinky whenever she got *impatient* with having all these hogs and not a single cow or horse. But a time or two when Dick was dropping cynical remarks about hogs, she could see it was all Ed could do to restrain himself.

The leg was a long time mending. Something in his knee refused to settle into place right, according to Dr. Roos; Ed would just have to look forward to having a game leg the rest of his life. Muriel took the news harder than Ed seemed to. He apparently thought he would be able to manage, and of couse he *would;* but she could hardly wait for Dick to be off on his own. Ed would manage beautifully in the long run, there was no doubt in her mind about that, even if it meant he would have a limp. But Dick had better find himself pretty soon or it would be too late. Whenever she tried to nudge him in the right direction, he would turn his sharp tongue on her. They didn't go visiting much, with Ed's leg the way it was. The three of them played a lot of seven-up or cooncan of an evening—or just Dick and she would play caroms as they had done when they were children. He could be great fun.

For a while, Ed used his leg as an excuse to stay home from church. She saw her chance, and when the time was ripe she launched her campaign to get them to switch to the Methodist Church in Ames. Her most telling argument was that Dick was already a member; she pinned everything on that, and she could see Ed was wavering. But right at the critical moment, Dick played her a dirty trick.

"I joined because I was chasing Stella Pritchard, you know

57

that, Sis, and I just never unjoined. Old Henshaw is the dullest preacher in central Kansas. So don't ask me to further your nefarious schemes."

Betrayed by her own brother! She could see by Ed's scowl that it would be months before she would dare bring the subject up again. She burst into tears, ran into their room, and threw herself on the double bed. Ed did not come to comfort her; leg or no leg, he should have tried; she would have forgiven him if he'd come to her. She could hear the chairs scrape up to the table. The men weren't saying anything, but she could feel they were against her by the way the cards slapped.

Then, the Saturday after Thanksgiving, Dick went off to a "buddies" party, veterans who had returned to Ames from Europe, and he got home after midnight when they were fast asleep. He banged and shouted and cursed. She had never seen a man so drunk. Her own brother! Thank goodness, they lived a quarter of a mile from their nearest neighbor, except for the Messerschmidts, whom they never saw. But the worst of it was that Ed, instead of calming him down, sort of joined him. He didn't get drunk, of course, because even if he'd wanted to they never had spirits in the house; but he did join Dick in ranting and going on in loud voices about how awful the world was. She ordered them to stop and go to bed, but they acted as though she hadn't said a word. She went to bed herself, but she couldn't help overhearing. She had never listened to such talk in her life. Here was Dick, a young man freshly home from sacrificing his hearing for his country, and he was raving about how awful airplanes were, and mustard gas, and cannon. Not just the Germans', but everybody's including ours. He said it was soul-killing, these weapons, and they'd killed his soul, he was dead already, and by "they" he didn't mean the Germans, he meant the American generals and politicians. And Ed, who had done everything his country asked him to do and made money out of it besides—here he was talking about the profit motive and the middleman as though they were agents of the devil. She was so sick and tired of hearing farmers talk about the middleman when they didn't know the first thing about business. Business was what made the country

58

rich and strong. And the Germans *started* the war. What was wrong with her men? Nobody ever used to talk like this, except Russian anarchists in big Eastern cities, like that one who shot President McKinley. She was so upset she was afraid she might lose this baby too.

The baby was a girl, and they named her Jane (after Muriel's mother) Hypatia (that was Ed's idea and she couldn't bring herself to oppose it). They called her Jenny, to be different; nobody they knew was called Jenny.

You could count on Dick to do everything wrong. He left for California, "to make his fortune," a week before Jenny was born. What timing! Of course it was a relief to have him off their hands, but if he was going to stay with them that long he might have stayed on till the big event had occurred. His own niece! But, if that's the way he wanted things, maybe it was just as well he'd gone when he had. Muriel did her part: she told him to look up Rosemary and Preston, and she wrote to them about Dick in terms that glowed as much as her conscience would let her make them glow.

Jenny was born two days after Prohibition went into effect, and that was surely a good omen. Muriel was even firmer than her mother about temperance: Prohibition was the best thing that had happened to America since Emancipation.

There seemed to be nothing wrong with Jenny when she was born, but Muriel did not have enough milk for her and no other kind seemed to agree with her. Weeks went by, and they tried every known formula, milk from three different cows, goat's milk even, but nothing worked. Dr. Roos told her not to worry about Jenny, she was colicky, as babies often were, but she wouldn't stay puny once she got over the colic. He also told Muriel it was nobody's fault she couldn't nurse Jenny; that was just nature's way sometimes, no one knew why. Her mother and women friends comforted her too. But Ed's sister Fran was dreadful. She was already on her second at the time, and she would nurse her wrinkled little hairy baby right in front of everybody—and beam. This was worse than uncouth, it went beyond bad man-

59

ners: she did it to let Muriel know what she was missing. Even so, Muriel could have been reconciled to being dry, if only Ed would say he forgave her for it. He never did. That meant he must be blaming her. He must think it was her fault Jenny was so sickly.

The worst part of it was that she knew it was her fault. But couldn't Ed have forgiven her anyway? He adored Jenny and was wonderfully gentle with her, as he was with all little creatures. Muriel could not bring herself to ask him for forgiveness, even though she wanted it so much, because it seemed to her that he loved Jenny more than he loved her. It was all right for a young mother to love her baby more than she loved her husband, for a few years anyhow; nature intended it. But Ed was a man; his first allegiance was to his wife, and nature intended him to protect her and their children equally. And Ed was a farmer too; she remembered the scorn in his voice when he had talked about a cow that had gone dry the year before. Oh, what had she done to deserve this dirty trick nature had played on her? It wasn't her fault she had so little milk, so why didn't he forgive her?

When Jenny was three months old, Owen and Fran—it would have to be them—got the scrawniest Jersey heifer anyone ever saw, and two months later she calved. That was the milk Jenny thrived on.

Well, thank the Lord something agreed with her.

By then, Muriel had lost interest in the farm almost entirely.

Ed was doing fine. She left him alone and devoted herself to Jenny, her girl friends, and her mother. They sewed together and exchanged recipes. On second Thursdays, unless something came up, one of them would give a report on some interesting current book on a cultural topic, such as ballet or the Hapsburgs or the religions of India. They talked babies and husbands and neighbors. This was the pattern of her years, and the one she wanted.

She kept putting on weight.

Two years later, she had their second, a strapping boy whom they named Eugene (after her father) Edward and called Gene. He was healthy from the start, though big and demanding, and

60

she doted on him. Ed of course was tickled pink to have a son, but the unexpected thing was that he took Jenny under his wing more than ever, downright spoiling her. Muriel felt a pang or two of jealousy for Gene's sake. But she was being silly; Ed was compensating, that was all. Meanwhile, though she had to devote most of her attention to the new one, she was careful to see to it that Jenny loved her baby brother as an older sister should.

Of course she couldn't nurse Gene either, and likewise of course Ed didn't say he didn't hold it against her, though he never blamed her by so much as a sniff.

Ed worked such long hours, she was thankful she had the babies to devote herself to. Whenever she felt cross with him for some little thing, she would remind herself how steady he was —the steadiest husband she knew. Mama adored him. He bought them a Model T Ford and a battery-set radio. He helped out with Mama financially, and this made all the difference; by taking in one boarder, Mama could stay in her own house where she had lived all her married life. He sometimes went over to Dunreith and played cards and drank home brew with "the boys"; but that was the only really serious fault he had, and she never let him forget what she, to say nothing of the law, thought of gambling and liquor. She had cured his sick headaches for him with good diet; it was just a matter of time till he quit drinking too. He had promised her he would have nothing to do with bootleggers. That was the first big step.

The women in her family had always had a tendency to put on weight, and after Jenny, Muriel had become the plumpest of all. Now, after Gene, she became downright stout. Dr. Roos said it was metabolism, and not to eat too much starch. She worked hard on dieting. She seldom took more than a cup of coffee for breakfast—a pity since breakfast was Ed's favorite meal. But she did so love to nibble. When Ed was around, she restrained herself, but, alone, she let herself pick at leftovers freely—after all, they shouldn't go to waste.

Something was missing. Every so often she felt a lack. But of what? This consciousness usually came to her during one of

61

those long, tedious sermons Baptists seemed to like, and for a while she thought it was the Episcopal services she was missing. Actually, she admired the zeal of the Baptists, narrow though it might be, and she could not pretend to herself that the Christmas and Easter services she attended with her mother at Trinity moved her in the way they used to before she was married. Ed said grace before every meal and of course that was right, and Muriel loved teaching Jenny to say her prayers—a little angel with golden curls. But Muriel almost never prayed on her own anymore. This was wrong of her, she knew that. But what good did praying do? That question was wrong too, but it kept floating in on the backwaters of her mind whether she liked it or not.

When she discovered she was pregnant for the fourth time, Ed slapped the table and said, with sparkling eyes, "That settles the matter, we've got to get a bigger house." She loved him when he was so decisive.

They discussed moving to another county, but they were both pretty halfhearted about it. Everything pointed in one direction: they should buy the Messerschmidt farm. It backed onto theirs, so if they just added it they would hardly have to move at all. The acreage was more than they needed, but the house was large and solid, brick, with a coal furnace. Mama, who had been increasingly troubled with quinsy, could come live with them if she felt like it. And the price was not exorbitant, not because the land was poor so much as because the Messerschmidts had not been liked in the neighborhood. They were standoffish —Muriel had never set foot inside their house nor they in hers —and they belonged to no church. When their only child, a son in college, died of infantile paralysis, nobody could blame them for wanting to move away; but it seemed peculiar for them to go all the way back to the old country, especially considering all the troubles going on in Germany. (Something was going wrong with the money, inflation, whatever that was.) Therefore, Muriel could persuade Ed to offer a good deal less than the price they were asking for the place. The farm had been for sale all winter, and it was nearly time for the spring plowing. The real

62

estate man from Bettancourt was discouraged about it, and he finally accepted Ed's offer, though he wasn't sure how the Messerschmidts would take it when they learned how little he had been able to get. Ed had no trouble getting a large mortgage on the place; in fact, the president of the Ames bank congratulated Ed personally on having driven such a hard bargain. When Ed told her this, he made a sour face, as though he didn't appreciate the compliment. So she didn't say much about the subject. The important thing was that he was acquiring some business sense at last.

That Thursday when she told the sewing circle they were going to move by the first of June, her mother looked at her radiantly and everyone congratulated her sincerely and warmly.

"You have everything that matters most in life," said Mrs. Roberts.

When Muriel knocked wood, Mrs. Roberts, who wore pince-nez and seldom smiled, leaned forward and grasped her wrist seriously.

"You must think of this as the high point of your life."

"Yes, but I wish they'd had another name."

Mrs. Steinhoff looked cross. "It's a good German name."

"Oh, I know," said Muriel, looking frantically for a way to get out of this trap she had got herself into, "I know, but it sounds so undignified *in English*."

"Oh, for heaven's sake," said her mother, "in five years the name Messerschmidt won't mean a thing to anybody. Call it the new place."

Two mornings later, her mother came down with pneumonia; and that afternoon the first of their hogs died of cholera. The vet said they were having an epidemic of cholera in Nebraska, a virulent form of it, too, but this was the first case he had heard of locally.

Six days later, the last of their hogs died; that same night her mother passed away.

The shock was more than Muriel could stand. She miscarried again.

63

Ed was as sympathetic with her as a man could be, but she was beyond caring. The doctor gave her sleeping syrup, and her sister took the children.

Ed said life must go on, and of course he was right. He said for her to take it easy till she felt up to scratch, they could move into the new house anytime; meanwhile, there was just one thing for him to do. Afterward, she realized that she should have discussed this with him at great length, for he was wrong and she half-knew it at the time. But she was so grief-stricken she couldn't pull herself together enough to do anything about it.

He mortgaged everything they owned to the hilt, had electricity brought in to the new place, built scientifically designed pens, and stocked them with the best breed of hog money could buy.

Their first night in the new house, in August, heavy snores in the attic woke Muriel up. She shook Ed, he heard the noise too. They had no doubt what it was, a man's snores, but of course when Ed went up with the lantern and his sawed-off shotgun, he found no one. Then that fall a woman's wail would drift along the eaves on the side of the house away from the barn. This happened three or four times, late at night, toward dawn. The snores only happened twice after Halloween, but both times they were loud. These noises bothered Ed as much as Muriel, and he was first to say the word: "ghosts."

What could possibly be more undignified than to be haunted by Messerschmidts? She persuaded Ed they shouldn't talk about it with anyone else until they were sure it wasn't their imaginations or something that could be fixed. They didn't want to become laughingstocks. Ed made things worse one evening at supper by pointing out that the wailing ghost couldn't have been a member of the Messerschmidt family since no Messerschmidt woman had died while they were occupying the house. They had lived here for fifteen years. Do you suppose they had had these ghosts all that time from the previous tenants and never mentioned it to anybody outside the family? No wonder they were

64

so queer. Ed and she looked at each other, and neither of them ate any more of the meal.

By winter, the bottom had dropped out of the hog market, and the next February the bank began foreclosure procedures. They would be left with their personal possessions and about $2,000.

Because the president of the bank was also a deacon in the Calvary Baptist Church in Ames and because he showed them no mercy, Ed vowed he would never set foot in another church in his life. Hypocrites, all of them. The biggest mistake he had ever made, and he'd made more than his share, was to even dream of becoming a missionary. From now on, he was going to worship God in His true church, the great outdoors, in the fields and woods. Money was the root of all evil.

She pretended to be scandalized by what he said against churches and she made it perfectly clear that she was going to remain a churchgoer all her life, but secretly she was pleased by his stand. For one thing, it meant she wouldn't have to go to the Bells' church any longer. For another, it made her realize that in this hour of trouble she did not want to turn to a minister for advice any more than Ed did.

Having no one else to turn to, they turned to each other. They had never been closer than now. Together again, she realized how far they had drifted apart. She thanked God: without these terrible troubles, they might never have become reunited.

Both of them knew without discussing the issue that they had to get away from Ames. But where to? Ed kept talking about Wyoming or Montana, some place where they could start over, a ranch of some sort, or he could get a job. The main thing was: a new start. And the word "ranch" kept coming up when he talked. Muriel agreed with him as hard as she could, but why couldn't they go where they knew at least one couple? Rosemary and Preston of course. She could tell from the way he balked that he was ashamed of being looked at as a failure by a man who was

65

successful in business, and she felt for him. But she couldn't face the future without at least one helping hand to reach for, just in case. Ed could be stubborn as a mule, and he was being stubborn now. She couldn't think how to get around him. She dropped an SLH or two in her letters to Rosemary.

Then Providence intervened.

One evening Fran and Owen—them again!—mentioned a fortune-teller they'd heard of, up in Beulah Center; she was supposed to be wonderful, half gypsy and half Cherokee, you couldn't beat that. Why didn't they all four of them go up some time and find out what she was like? Ed snorted, and Muriel pooh-poohed the notion. But the next day she brought it up with him seriously. The two of them might just go privately, purely out of curiosity, an outing for them. He scowled and shifted in his chair and scratched the underside of his thigh, but he agreed.

As they were leaving for Beulah Center, they stopped by the mailbox at the foot of the lane, and this was where Fate came in. There was only one letter, from Rosemary, and Muriel read it aloud as they drove along. Preston and his uncle Rupert had just bought a prune ranch not too far from Santa Rosa and would Ed consider coming to work it for them? If he would, Preston would like it better than anything. As for Rosemary herself: "If we're *such* good friends at 2,000 miles, what will we be at 20? A hundred times as good?" Rosemary had also included a brochure of The Native Sons of the Golden West, which said, among other things, that God had made California to be a paradise for the white man. "What hogwash," said Ed, and Muriel had to giggle. But she could tell by the way he was clenching his jaw as he steered that he was seriously considering the possibility of taking Preston up on his offer.

Madame Szazlo had black eyes and a sharp, thin nose, and she spoke with a strange accent, slurring, insinuating. She talked with them both together for a while and inspected their hands. Then she pulled back the curtain to the inner sanctum and told Muriel to come in with her. The only light in there was from two scented candles. Muriel's heart thumped, and she was grateful that Ed was near at hand. Madame Szazlo peered into her crystal

66

ball and muttered so that Muriel had to strain: she saw Muriel far away, standing by an ocean, surrounded by white flowers, happy. California!

Driving off, she could hardly wait to ask Ed what Madame Szazlo had told him. He had been walking in a vineyard picking grapes; strange dark grapes, big ones; the vines towered above his head. . . . What could they possibly be but prune plums!

Ed scoffed when she brought "providential" into it, but her enthusiasm was too much for him. (Thank heaven, Rosemary had used the word "ranch" in her letter. Muriel dropped Providence and Fate and dwelt on prune *ranch*.) By the time they got home, he agreed the best thing for them to do was to move to California and take over the ranch.

No more hogs. No more of the Bell clan. And a heavenly climate. At the end of March, with the temperature down near zero but no snow on the ground, they piled everything they could into the Model-T, shipping the rest by freight train, and headed west.

3

Mother

Things began to come to a head with Gene's graduation from high school. It didn't seem reasonable to Muriel that his graduating could have started anything, but it was the first important event to happen along about then. Things did change, that was undeniable, so something must have caused it. She strove to understand.

The longer she lived the more convinced she was that everything that happened had a meaning. Her first full realization of how this must be the case had come to her six years before. At that time, 1933, the Depression was at its worst, gangsters had wrecked Prohibition, and Roosevelt had pushed through Repeal —a terrible year. One of the members of the Montezuma Ladies Club had got a Jesuit priest, who was visiting nearby in Geyserville, to come speak to them. Father O'Horgan was a professor of philosophy at the University of San Francisco and such a cultivated and humorous man. It had simply not occurred to Muriel before that a priest could have a highly developed sense of

68

humor. But there was nothing funny about his message: *we must never forget that everything means something in God's mind; everything hangs together.* As soon as he said it, she realized that she had always believed it without knowing she did. *To understand how things hang together is to praise God.* She would redouble her efforts to understand. She was almost glad that San Francisco was seventy-five miles away and across the Golden Gate, because she admired Father O'Horgan far more than any Protestant minister she had ever met, even though he was bald and tubby, and she was so thirsty for more of his wisdom that she might well have succumbed and gone to Catholic services when he was preaching, just to partake. She was glad she didn't have to put Ed to that test. Oh, Ed often would say that one church was bad as another, but she knew he didn't mean it. Dr. Jackson of the Montezuma Community Church was ordained a Methodist, and anybody could tell what he was going to do and say next. Ed once observed that he had no use for him, but the voice in which he said it was comfortable, neighborly. But who could guess what a Roman Catholic priest might do, might say? All the terrible deeds those Popes and Inquisitors had perpetrated— they weren't to be trusted. Still, *things hang together.* She had seen Father O'Horgan only that once, six years ago, but he still popped up in her dreams from time to time.

Something else important had happened that year, at a pre-Christmas party with Rosemary and Preston to celebrate Repeal —the men's idea naturally. If anybody other than Rosemary had said such a thing to her, she could have risen above it, but it was her own friend, in her own living room.

For some reason, at about ten o'clock Ed and Preston decided they had to go to the creek down at the back of the orchard and see how much water was in it; the night happened to be foggy but not too cold; they could be heard in the distance, shouts and laughter. The good Lord only knew what the children were thinking. The McPhersons had brought their two boys, and all four children were supposed to be asleep. Fat chance of that, with their fathers misbehaving so loudly!

Then all of a sudden Rosemary leaned forward—she'd

69

drunk two glasses of wine at dinner, there was that to be taken into consideration—and said in a low *husky* voice, not her own voice at all, that no matter how peeved she ever got with Preston she would always have to forgive him because of the marvelous way he filled her so. Muriel, naturally assuming that Rosemary meant he *ful*filled her, was about to say how lovely it was to see people so happily married, when Rosemary did something that made her realize, No, it wasn't fulfilled, it was *filled*.

"Sometimes," Rosemary said leaning back and half-closing her eyes, "I can feel him clear up to here." She put her hands flat on each side of her chest, high, then slid them down over her bosom. They held her breasts, actually squeezed them.

Muriel was so shocked she was at a loss for words. But, if she didn't say something, she would have to bolt out into the fog herself. But, if she did that, Rosemary would run after her, and what about the children *then*? She burst into chatter, on and on about Father O'Horgan, without really paying attention to her words, and before long Rosemary was back to normal, her hands back in her lap where they ought to be and her eyes open.

It hadn't happened.

That was the only sure way to handle such an episode. They never mentioned the subject again, and Rosemary never had another lapse of the sort in Muriel's presence.

Nevertheless, Muriel could not put it out of her mind completely. Bad enough to have to talk to the doctor about female complaints, but to talk to *any*body about *that!* She had never even thought about it, not really. But now she couldn't help doing so. Ed didn't fill her. Whatever it was, it wasn't *filling*. Besides, they never did that anymore. For years, she had been successfully rising above the whole thing. And here Rosemary— her best friend—had set her to thinking about it against her will. If it didn't fill her, then what did it do? She knew from experience how much easier it was to keep a thing in its place once she had found *the* word for it. But for this she couldn't find the right word, if one existed. What was she thinking, *if* one existed. In God's mind there was a word for everything. The whole perplexity nagged at her off and on for months, till she remembered

70

something Father O'Horgan had said: "Sometimes our problem is that we haven't put the question the right way." Of course. She had got hold of things by the wrong end. The question was not: Since that didn't fill her, what did it do? The question was: What had ever truly filled her? And to this there was only one answer, her babies.

Once this understanding came to her, many things cleared up, especially pertaining to Rosemary. Muriel had always been bothered a little by the McPhersons' casualness about their children. They either disciplined them too severely or not enough— Preston was worse than Rosemary about this. They both seemed to ignore the children for long stretches, but every once in a while they would come to and heap affection on them, smother them with it. Whereas with her and Ed, not a day passed, even now with Jenny off at junior college, but what they talked over at least one little thing concerning each of the children. Her babies had filled her before they were born, and what filled her now was her babies still. She made a point of reminding Rosemary, in a thousand little ways, that the center of every woman's life was her family, and "the family exists for the sake of the child"—she had read that in a woman's magazine. It was true.

Meanwhile, Gene's graduation was coming up. Such a big, gawky boy, but manly. Ed complained that she doted on him. All right! It was *because* she doted on him that she worried over him. He was beginning to behave so strangely in so many ways; he was bumptious and uncouth, even with his own mother.

Gene stood eighth in a graduating class of nearly two hundred. He was a double letterman, one letter for being a forward on the varsity basketball team (he was six feet three) and the other for the standing broad jump. For this event, he took first place in the Redwood League two years in a row.

And last but not least, the evening before the ceremony itself, he was going to appear as the second male lead in the senior class play. Hildur Torelli, the wife of the drama coach—he was an English teacher who directed plays as an outside activity for the pupils—told Muriel confidentially that she was sure her hus-

71

band regretted that he hadn't cast Gene for the lead, he was *so* much better than the boy who was playing it. Everything was pointing to a grand occasion, and Muriel was bursting with pride. So was Ed, though he didn't show it; but she knew how proud he must be feeling deep inside.

The graduation ceremony was set for June 19. Knowing that she had quite a bout of persuading ahead of her, she started in the middle of May.

"Honey, why don't we think of inviting Rosemary and Preston to Gene's graduation?"

He snorted.

"It would be so nice for them to see him in the play, and we haven't got together with them for years."

"Two years, to be exact, the time of Jenny's graduation. I told you then and I tell you now: if I never see Preston McPherson again as long as I live, that'll be soon enough for me. You can go down and see Rosemary all you want, and you can have her up here, but don't drag Preston and me in on it."

She dropped the subject for a week. He would come around. What Preston had done was bad but not *that* bad.

"Now, Ed, Memorial Day is not far off, and we just have to make up our minds about Rosemary and Preston."

"I've made up my mind and you know how."

"Aren't you even going to see Jenny graduate?"

"Not if I can help it."

Jenny was finishing up in Santa Rosa Junior College, and of course a J.C. graduation didn't mean very much. Still, it meant something. She was in the upper third of her class, and if she got a good summer job and saved up, she would be able to go to San Francisco State and get her B.A. degree and teach; or she might go to nursing school and become a registered nurse. Jenny kept saying she wanted her parents to come to the ceremony, and of course Muriel wouldn't have missed it for the world. But Ed had been getting worse and worse over the years about traveling, even driving the twenty-odd miles to Santa Rosa. The only time he would drive in to the "city"—he called it a city though

72

really it was just an overgrown town—was when he absolutely had to get something for the ranch.

Muriel didn't think it mattered all that much whether he attended the J.C. graduation, but, up to a couple of days beforehand, she was going to pretend that it did. Then her plan was to make a trade: "You don't have to go to Jenny's graduation if you'll let Rosemary *and* Preston come to Gene's." She wasn't silly enough to put it so bluntly, but that's what it would amount to.

The first sign that all might not be well was when the McPhersons were late. Rosemary had written that they hoped to get to the Bells' house in time for a quick bite; but, as Ed pointed out when Muriel began to stew at their not arriving, all it would take was a flat tire. That soothed her spirits considerably, and left her only one real regret, that Jenny would miss the play. Preston—generous as always—had given Jenny a summer job in his office, and naturally they were all three coming together. They couldn't leave till after work, and "the best laid schemes o' mice and men . . ." Well, Rosemary and Preston would manage to survive if they missed a high school farce, though Jenny ought to enjoy seeing her brother "onstage."

But Muriel had not reckoned on the play itself. Not only was it bad and most of the performances worse, but the fact that the leading girl's acting was good was the crowning insult. The play was called *A Thief There Was*, and the situation was risqué enough to call for careful handling. The first ("real") husband of a woman who has divorced him and remarried comes to steal her back from her second ("legal") husband. Weeks before, when Muriel had picked up from Gene what the play was about, Hildur Torelli had reassured her that it was all perfectly harmless. In fact the words looked harmless enough, as Muriel learned by prompting Gene as he was memorizing his part—she insisted on doing it and he said he appreciated her help. But because of the leading "actress" nothing was as it should have been.

Theda Barry was her name, and she ogled like a movie star;

73

she made her voice slinky. But what could you expect of a girl whose mother would name her after that shameless vamp Theda Bara? So common. Gene played the first husband, the one who tries and fails to steal her back, and, stiff and unnatural as he was, the other boy, the lead, was worse. But Muriel thought it was *good* for children to be awkward on stage, especially when they were playing grown-up parts in a risqué farce, for their self-consciousness would keep everybody, offstage and on, from taking the situation seriously. From reading the play several times, she knew that the first husband was supposed to be a black villain, the second husband a knight in shining armor, and the wife a damsel in distress torn between sinful and dutiful love. But Theda was so convincing, and so suggestive, that everything altered. She made it seem that the wife was conniving with the first husband not out of love of any kind but in order to make her second husband jealous, more attentive to her. The baggage!

The low point came right before the intermission. The curtain closed slowly on Gene and Theda as they were clasped in a kiss. Muriel could feel in her vitals that they were not just acting, they were really kissing. The moment the curtain dropped, the applause that broke out was downright vulgar—catcalls, wolf whistles, shouts—and as the audience was filing out for a breath of fresh air, she overheard one callow, pimply, towering boy say to another, "Say, that was really hot, wasn't it?" Her eyebrows went up and her nostrils flared.

Ed didn't utter a peep. Somehow, in his suit, which he had worn at their wedding and was too big for him now, he seemed shrunken and old.

"What's the matter, honey?" she said. "You look as though you'd swallowed a dill pickle whole."

"I wish I had. It'd pass eventually."

"Ed!"

"Let's go home."

"Ed!"

"Gene can get himself a ride."

"We don't want to hurt his feelings."

74

"He's hurt more than my feelings."

"People would notice."

"Let them think what they want. I know what I think of them. There's too many, and they stink like hogs. I'm sweltering. Put your hand up under my coat and feel my shirt."

It was drenched, to be sure, but her first impulse was to say, "What about me? I have to wear a corset." However, there was more satisfaction in not complaining about herself—and not sympathizing with him either. She gave an indifferent little shrug, glancing around for someone to wave to. Spotting no one she knew, she turned back to Ed and said in a placating voice, "Honey, don't you want to see how the play comes out?"

The scowl he gave her! She couldn't remember a look so ferocious since the first day they arrived in Twin Creek Valley. Preston had been laid up with a bout of catarrh when they had arrived in Santa Rosa, and his uncle Rupert was down in San Francisco on business. So they had driven to Twin Creek Valley and the prune ranch by themselves. The day was hot and dry; the trees were not at all impressive-looking, scraggly and uneven; the water in the creek down in back was muddy. But the straw that broke the camel's back was the four-room frame house with two broken windows, a rickety porch, and a screen door with the screen pushed through—their home-to-be. The paint was in better condition than you would expect, but an ugly color— shit brown, Ed said, right in front of her and the children. He stamped around so ferociously, beating his thigh with his hand every so often, muttering curses she didn't dare reprove him for, slamming the door on the barn, overturning a rusty harrow, scowling as though the day of wrath was at hand, that she had to bury her own disappointment—mercifully—in order to protect the children and try to calm him down. And here he was scowling the same way because of a crowd of youngsters and a silly play.

"That boy," he said in a harsh voice, right in the middle of the throng—thank God he hadn't said Gene, so people would not know whom he meant. "That boy is headed for a life of sin."

75

It was unfair of him to say such a thing in circumstances where she couldn't get back at him. All she could do was give him a firm nudge with her elbow. She took a haughty stance and made herself look about serenely.

And there came Jenny, right in the nick of time.

Standing in a side doorway, waving her freckled arms, Jenny in her white organdy graduation dress appeared to her mother a vision, an angel of rescue. Not that there was anything angelic about Jenny physically, only her smile, her radiant smile.

Jenny was taller than Ed by two inches, and she had the Storr women's tendency toward heftiness. (Since they had moved to California, Muriel had not told a living soul how much she weighed. Four years ago, she had had to quit going to Dr. Baum, much as she trusted him, because he had been so unkind about her weight problem. As though she could do anything about metabolism, which is what the doctors agreed it was. And now Jenny, with at least thirty extra pounds already.) The heavy round frames of the new glasses Jenny had got that winter made her round face look rounder yet, and her straw-brown hair was even more tousled than usual. But she was so radiant and alive. Muriel's desperation ebbed away, for not only could Jenny cajole her father into anything (so long as it didn't involve his having to travel farther than Montezuma), but she was utterly reliable. The senior class nickname for her had been The Rock of Gibraltar. She'd brayed like a donkey when she'd told this to her family, and when Muriel, seeing the hurt in her eyes, had shown indignation—after all, the Rock of Gibraltar might be reliable but it is not exactly tiny—Jenny had only laughed the louder.

But if Muriel was happy and relieved to see her, Ed acted like a drowning man who has just caught hold of a raft. When she reached them, laughing and giving a happy little shriek, his arms clamped her, all but squeezing the breath out of her.

"Well, daughter. Well, daughter."

"Papa! Goodness! Ow!"

"Now, Ed," said Muriel, "remember where we are."

He took the women by their upper arms. "Let's go home."

76

"Aw, Paw, I want to see the play. That's what I came for." Ed looked about, as though for a place to spit.

"Now, Papa," said Muriel, "public places." He hrrmphed. "We have to stay for Gene's sake."

"Is it that bad?" Jenny whispered, leaning forward.

"Worse," said Ed.

"There are many interesting things about it," said Muriel firmly, "and we haven't seen the second half yet. Where are Preston and Rosemary?"

"We had two flat tires!" Jenny clapped her hands and hopped. "Can you imagine that?" Three girls she had known in high school yoohooed and waved. She waved back but did not try to leave her parents. Besides, Ed had not let go of her arm. "Preston was so dirty by the time he got the second one changed that he couldn't have come here even if he wanted to, which he sure didn't. Rosemary was going to, only when we drove into town guess who was standing in front of Goodman's with that same old crazy suitcase? You know, where the Greyhound bus stops? Uncle Dick!"

"Oh, lord," said Muriel.

"It never rains but it pours," said Ed, but he did not look altogether displeased.

"So, anyway, they all three went to Twin Creek, and I said we'd come along as soon as the play got out."

Sitting through the rest of the performance, Muriel worked hard to keep her mind off the play. At least Gene did not have to kiss Theda Barry again; but when she ogled him, he ogled right back, and that was nearly as bad as the kiss had been. What had Mr. Torelli been thinking of?

Dick. What strange lands had he gone to this time? India again? To think that not once in all the years they had lived in California had any of Ed's relatives bothered them but only her own sailor of a brother. Every two or three years he would show up and stay for a few days, or once, when he wasn't feeling well, for a month. Of course he brought unusual presents for them all, especially for the children, and told wild stories that nobody

77

could help enjoying—*and* he would disappear with Ed out in the barn where the wine keg was stored in a manger. The very first visit Dick had made twelve years ago, she had absolutely put her foot down about his language: he was not to use bad words in front of her or the children ever. When she told him this, he looked as though he could bite her nose off, but any child of their Mama's knew that this requirement was no more than right. He never once lapsed into anything worse than an occasional damn or hell. Once he mentioned scarlet ladies. Jenny, ten or eleven at the time, was listening to him wide-eyed, and of course she couldn't have had the faintest idea what scarlet ladies meant; but, with a crook of Muriel's little finger, it was passed over so smoothly that Jenny didn't even ask.

The last time Jenny had been home from J.C., at Easter, she said they mustn't buy anything made in Japan, like silk stockings, because of the invasion of Manchuria. Or made in Germany, because of the Nazis.

Germany causing trouble again. What was there about the Germans? And the Communists weren't content to have Russia for themselves, they were pushing in everywhere.

Gene hadn't been able to find a job for the summer. He hadn't got into serious trouble yet, but some of his friends . . . Motorcycles.

She had been reelected president of the Montezuma Ladies Club; this would make her third consecutive term. There were some lovely women in the club, but it was stuck in a rut. She must find some way to breathe new life into it. Not that she cared too terribly; it was all just for fun really. She had been surprised at how calmly she had taken Jenny's proclamation the summer before, "I will never join a women's club." At the moment Jenny said that, she had been in a peeve, and it was true she wasn't a joiner, yet; but time would tell. To Muriel, the important thing was that Jenny was clearly going to devote her life to others. "I thank Thee, Lord, for this my daughter Jane Hypatia whom Thou has vouchsafed me for my joy and my support. Amen." She reached over and gave Jenny's hand an affectionate squeeze. Jenny glanced at her and squinched up her eyes.

78

At least Dick's being there this evening along with Preston would ease things all around, what with Ed so touchy and proud.

She was set to find alcohol on Dick's breath, and because she did find it and because he was obviously glad to see her—"Well, Sis, how they been treating you?"—she did not realize how much he had changed until she was hugging him.

"Dick?" She held him at arm's length. His neck was scrawny as a picked chicken's. "You're a shadow of yourself."

"I could use twenty or thirty pounds, hch hch. If you've got any to spare."

"Oh, Dick." Tears came to her eyes. "You've been sick."

"Two months in a Singapore hospital," he said out of the side of his mouth, with a W. C. Fields drawl, "teetering on the brink of the grave."

"Honestly?" Jenny squealed. Her eyes were wide; her lips were trying not to grin. "What did you have?"

"An unnamed tropical fever."

Muriel gasped. "Unnamed!"

"Don't fret yo' fat, Sister, I can't give you any because I left it all behind."

"Dick! How could you suspect me of such a thing? I wasn't worried about catching it."

"You damn well ought to have been, because, I tell you, it makes you rue the day you were ever born."

"I was thinking how awful it must have been for you."

"Thanks," he drawled. "It was."

She could not deny that she was relieved to learn he wasn't contagious, but she was so ashamed to have been thinking of herself first at such a moment that she sobbed, "Oh, Dick," and wept a little.

On previous visits, he and Ed would grasp each other's hard, weathered right hands when they first met and have a sort of friendly squeezing contest which, on purpose, neither ever won. But now, Ed, without a word, took Dick by the shoulders and hugged him awkwardly, pressing his cheek against Dick's.

Dick's clothes were loose on him, his hair was thinner than

79

ever, his left eyelid drooped, and Ed's affection obviously moved him. Muriel overflowed with emotion and wept a little more.

When the men separated, she said to Dick, "At least there aren't any permanent complications?"

"Only one," he answered, jaunty again. He tapped his chest with his left thumb. "The old ticker."

Jenny glurked and ran into the house. Muriel wanted to follow her, wanted to press Dick to her bosom, wanted to break down and cry hard, wanted to faint. She stood there immobile.

Rosemary, who had remained in the background with Preston, came up to her now, and the women hugged one another and exchanged usual greetings with unusual intensity. Out of the corner of her eye, Muriel saw Ed and Preston shake hands and say hello like the old friends they were.

She wished she could take her corset off. "I'm feeling a bit dizzy," she said in an undertone, and Rosemary helped her into the house. But, reluctant to mention her corset even to Rosemary, she refused to let her help her into the bedroom but sat at the kitchen table saying she felt much better, just fine now—and a glass of cool water *did* make her feel better.

Rosemary took over and did exactly the right thing: she put on water for coffee, set the table, took out the spice cake Muriel had made that afternoon, chatted, made everyone feel natural. It could have been such a strained occasion; instead, she made it a family reunion, and Muriel, watching her with a glazed smile, did not in any way feel reproved for having fallen down on the job. Rosemary had only one fault in Muriel's eyes: she had too much cheer sometimes, and it was more than slightly affected. But Muriel was grateful for it now and resolved never to tease Rosemary again about dyeing her hair.

Dick was resting on the chesterfield in the front room; they were to get him up when coffee and cake were ready.

Preston and Ed were sitting at the table across from her. Seated like this so you couldn't see how "broad in the beam" Preston was, he looked like a distinguished man: rimless bifocals, high forehead, erect posture, firm jawline despite a slight tendency to jowliness. His worst fault was that his voice was rather grating in quality and he often spoke too loud. He had a hearty laugh, which could be raucous and raspy too.

Three years before, Preston's Uncle Rupert had announced that he was beginning to retire. A widower with no children, he was going to leave his half of the partnership to Preston. However, before he died, he wanted to give away a good deal to other relatives, in order to avoid inheritance taxes, and he wanted to sell his share of the properties that he and Preston owned jointly. Preston, who of course wanted to keep only the best investments, would have to sell most of them to raise enough money to buy Rupert's share of the rest. He had decided to sell the Twin Creek Valley prune ranch.

It was true that the ranch had not been a paying proposition, seldom clearing enough from the sales of prunes to cover taxes, upkeep, and the salary Preston faithfully paid Ed. The salary was just enough for the Bells to scrape by on, but at least they had never had to go on relief or WPA.

Preston had explained all this to Ed very carefully and tactfully, and Ed had, to Muriel's deep approval, told Preston they were indebted to him for his loyal generosity during these hard times more than words could ever say. It was a delicate moment; the four of them had been seated at this same table, around the kerosene lamp, the children in bed; Rosemary was looking at her folded hands, and Muriel's eyes were swimming. But Preston, when Ed had expressed their gratitude, instead of thanking him or mumbling something or even just being silent as friends can be at such a moment, burst out into a bray of laughter and told Ed not to be a fool, it was all just business.

Muriel had been as shocked as though Preston had thrown ice water into her face. Rosemary had glared Preston down and then gone on to smooth things over as best she could. Ed had closed up like a fist.

Afterward, Rosemary did not make the mistake of apologizing to Muriel for Preston's behavior. On the contrary, next morning while they were making breakfast, she spoke in a furious voice of his stupid, crude habit of laughing to cover up when he was em-

81

barrassed; she'd tried to break him of it a thousand times, and he always relapsed. Muriel murmured sympathetically. It made her feel better to think of the serious discussions that were going to be taking place behind the closed doors of the McPhersons' bedroom in evenings to come.

A year later, when Rosemary and Preston had come back for Jenny's high school graduation, Ed was down with an attack of Bright's disease and his game leg was bothering him. He could barely hobble, moaning and groaning, to the ceremony. Muriel had seen his leg go out on him to suit his own convenience more than once, but Dr. Baum said his kidney condition (Dr. Baum called it nephritis) needed careful watching; she could not hold his illness against Ed this time. Still, she had been suspicious, because it kept him from having to chat with Preston. Luckily for both men, Ed had some business to occupy the five minutes politeness required them to spend together. He had mentioned to an Italian winegrower higher up the valley that there had been no buyers for the prune ranch, and the Italian, Al Flattigatti, said maybe he'd be interested. Preston had gone up to talk with Al that same afternoon, and a few times during the two years since, Al had dropped by and talked with Ed.

"Say, Ed." Preston had a "business voice" and was using it now. "Al Flattigatti was down last week and he came by with his lawyer. I think we're going to work out a deal."

"That a fact."

"Yes, he wants to pull the trees and plant a new variety of grape."

"Well, Muriel," said Ed, "it looks like we're going to move at last."

"Not unless you want to," said Preston. "Part of the deal is that you stay on here. I wouldn't close it otherwise. Al knows how reliable you are. As for myself," he started to laugh but caught Rosemary's eye and choked instead, "well, you found the buyer for me, you saved me the real estate broker's five percent, I want you to know I'm grateful for that."

Dick appeared in the doorway behind Preston.

82

"This ranch," Preston went on, "I thought I was going to lose my shirt on it, and you came to the rescue, Ed." This time he brayed. "Saved by the Bell."

"On October 24, 1927," Dick drawled, coming up to the table, "at eight fifteen in the evening, in a pub in East London, I heard a worse pun than that. And once in the trenches in 1918, only I lost track of the exact day, but I'm sure it was late morning and drizzly, I heard another pun worse than that. Preston, keep on trying. The man who can make a pun as lousy as that can make a worse one if he just sticks with it."

Jenny laughed for everybody.

Car, shouts, and in burst Gene, yelling, "Hey, Pop, can I borrow the Model A?"

"Genie!" said his mother.

"Hi, Mom."

"Just look who's here, sweetie."

"Oh, hi, Aunt Rosemary, hi, Uncle Preston." Then his whole manner lightened. "It's Uncle Dick! Doggone, how are you?" Gene, a head taller than Dick, hugged and thumped him, repeating, "Doggone, son of a gun."

Muriel settled back in her corset, comfortable for the first time in hours, and felt her normal spirits being restored.

After the greetings, Gene, all wrought up, turned back to Ed. "Can I have the car, Pop? We want to have a cast party and go down to the beach, you know, drive down along the Russian River to Jenner and roast wienies and stay up all night, and we need a car. Can I?"

"All right, my boy," said Ed. "It's a big occasion for you."

"Swell," Gene cried. "Where's the key?"

"Who'll be the chaperone?" asked Muriel.

"Mr. Torelli. He's going to bring the cider."

"Who's going to bring the beer?" said Dick.

"Richard! Shame on you," said Muriel, "for putting ideas in the boy's head."

"Eugene," said Dick, "take that idea out of your head right this minute."

83

"Look," said Gene, "can I? There's five kids out there in Pat's car now and the rumble seat won't open."

"Here." Ed gave him the key.

"One minute, young man," said Muriel. "The least you can do is introduce your friends to your family."

"Do I have to?"

"You certainly do."

Theda was wearing a cream-colored skirt and a blue sleeveless blouse, saddle shoes and pink bobby socks, and no lipstick. Her black hair was in a cute bob, and she was quiet and polite. Everything about her was demure, completely unlike the impression she had made in the play, except for her eyes, which had heavy lids and long lashes and which would not be deceived. The others were boys who had been to the house before.

"Well," said Ed when they had driven off, "that was a surprise."

"And a pleasant one," said Muriel.

"What an interesting face that girl has," said Rosemary. "I never saw eyes like that."

"She's a Digger," said Jenny and laughed.

"A what?" said Muriel.

"The Gold Digger of 1939," said Dick.

"No," said Jenny, "her father was a Digger Indian."

"Oh, my God," said Rosemary.

"What about her mother?" said Muriel.

"She's white. She runs a diner down on 101, half a mile north of Weedport."

"Where's the Indian?" said Ed.

"Who knows?" Jenny scowled. "What's wrong with being an Indian, anyway? They were here first."

Ed looked out the window into the dark and made chewing motions.

"Of course, dear," said Muriel to smooth things over. "I hope the children have a lot of fun tonight. They'll be so tired for graduation tomorrow morning, but one night up late won't hurt them. It's such a relief to see what a nice girl Theda really is. In numbers there is safety."

84

"Five to one is Digger's fun," said Preston and brayed.

Dick muttered under his breath, "Try again, ass." Muriel, sitting next to Dick, gave his foot a cautionary nudge with hers. He said he hoped he wouldn't spoil the party but he had to go to bed.

Muriel was so exhausted by the events of the day that she expected to drop off to sleep, as usual, the instant her head touched the pillow. Instead, her eyes flew open, and she lay in the dark listening to Ed's breathing turn shallow, then regular and deep. She tried to fasten her thoughts onto Dick; he must stay with them till he was fully recovered, that was clear. But she could not keep her thoughts from wandering to the young people on the beach. Mr. Torelli was probably not much of a chaperon; he was still under thirty himself, and Hildur would be home with the baby.

Then, in her mind's eye, she saw Gene kissing Theda as vividly as when she had seen them do it on stage. She tried not to watch them, but had to; the curtains started to draw closed; not till Gene and Theda were hidden from view, could she attach her mind to other thoughts. She told herself Theda was a nice girl, really; but those dark, steady eyes kept troubling her. But then, if Theda was fast, what about Gene? Boys were different but not that different. Besides, Gene knew better, he had been brought up; and poor Theda . . . There they were again, kissing, and she had to watch them till the curtains slowly closed. She cried, but quietly so as not to wake up Ed. He would try to comfort her, but she didn't want to be comforted, she wanted to cry herself to sleep.

In the middle of the night, she came to with a start, sat up in bed, and said out loud, "Yes, what is it?" Ed grunted and turned over. The loud voice she had heard was not that of any man she knew; it was a voice with a beard. She felt her heart pounding. Words echoed in her head, remote and clear: "Thou shalt feel what thou shouldst feel."

"All right," she said to herself, "I shall, yes." She went back to sleep in peace.

85

Except for Gene, the summer seemed to be shaping up well. Dick moved into Jenny's old room. "I'm going to hibernate, Sis. This is what is known as summer hibernation." He began to improve immediately, visibly. Poor wandering soul, how could anybody get well without a home? She kept tempting him with nourishing goodies which she cooked up; but she would overestimate his appetite and usually have to finish them herself; there were so many dishes Ed didn't like that he seldom helped with Dick's leftovers, and Gene almost never ate dinner or supper at home with them. She was gaining again, alarmingly. She promised herself to go on a strict diet as soon as Dick left.

Al Flattigatti came by toward the end of June, and she got acquainted with him for the first time. If you overlooked his heavy accent, he seemed more like a businessman than a farmer. He had handsome gray hair, he was wearing a starched white shirt, and he treated her with respect. He smoked the worst-smelling cigars any man had ever inflicted on her, and many a man had done just that, beginning with her father—his only bad habit. So many men seemed to think cigar-smoking was the he-man thing to do, and she supposed it was. Thank goodness, Ed just smoked roll-your-own cigarettes, except that he would join Al, out of politeness, when Al offered him a stogey. At least Ed didn't chew the rancid butt as Al did.

Addressing her, Al said he was on his way back from Santa Rosa where all the papers had been signed, sealed, and delivered, and he had come by to explain his plans to them. Then he turned to Ed. Once the vintage was in that fall and the prunes were dried, they would pull all the trees and plant a sturdy new vine the Agriculture School at Davis had developed, and then, when those vines were well established, they would graft a wine grape onto the stock—lots of good red wine. He would bring in electricity and a phone to the house and deepen the well, and he would pay Ed $100 a month, over and above the house rent-free as before. He wanted Ed to know that one of the attractions of the place for him had been having Ed there to run it. Preston had told him how Ed hadn't been able to make a success of it with

86

the prunes. But Al wanted Ed *anyhow*. Ed was affable and hearty, and thanked him. But after he left, Ed, without a word, but with a sour look on his face, went out into the orchard for the rest of the afternoon by himself. Muriel decided not to influence his decision in any way but to let him work it out by himself. She could rely on him to do what had to be done. They would be able to afford another car now, for her to get about in as she pleased, and that would be some compensation to her for living on property where wine grapes were being grown—that and Ed's having such a sensible, considerate man as Mr. Flattigatti to work for.

Jenny had got acquainted with a man-wife team of doctors, clients of Preston's. Their name was Spratt, he an obstetrician and she a pediatrician, and of course Dick couldn't resist: "Betwixt them both, they lick the platter clean." Their daughter Eileen, who had been a registered nurse for five years, explained to Jenny why she had decided not even to try to be a doctor. "Nurses help people the same as doctors," Jenny told them Eileen had said to her, "but they don't have so many ways to make big mistakes. And oh, people are so grateful. That's what Eileen does it for, the gratitude in their eyes. And that's why I'm going to do it too. I'm going to nursing school in the fall." "Well, at least you know the reason and it's a good one," said Ed. "I'm so happy for you, dear," said her mother.

But Gene. The day after graduation he got a job working from noon till midnight five days a week in a filling station in Weedport. It only paid thirty-two cents an hour, but at least it would tide him over the summer. But then, at the end of the first week when he got paid, it turned out that he actually collected only sixteen cents an hour, because the owner was holding the other half to pay for a motorcycle which Gene was buying from him on time. Ed and Muriel discovered all this only when, on his first day off, he came home riding the machine—a big red Indian that made a terrible racket. The owner had made him put in a week of work before he could take possession. He seldom got home before one or two in the morning. One of his days off in

87

July when it was hot as sin, he and some buddies of his rode their "bikes" clear to Sacramento—to see a movie, he said; he got home at three in the morning. He usually found time to play a game of checkers with Dick before he hroomed off to work. Gene got along with his uncle a hundred times better than he did with his parents. "Join the twentieth century," he would say to his father, chuckling as though it was a joke when it wasn't. With his mother, he was too polite, hastening to agree with anything she said but then with a smile sliding away.

Once, resting, she found herself accidentally eavesdropping on a checker game between Gene and Dick on the screened porch, and she thought she heard "Theda." But she was not sure and she didn't want to press the issue. However, a couple of days later, she stopped by the diner half a mile above Weedport, just to have a look around. It was a railroad car with the wheels off, set up on railroad ties. There was a whitewashed shack in back, and the ground was bare, with dusty weeds here and there, and a clump of elephant-ear cactus. She ordered iced tea. There was no one in the place except the woman behind the counter. After she had served Muriel, she leaned on the other end of the counter on both elbows reading a pulp magazine. She looked bitter and tired; her slip showed in back. Unable to think of a good way to start a conversation, Muriel drank up and left.

By the end of August, she felt desperate about Gene. He had turned surly. He kept borrowing money from his father and "forgetting" to pay it back, and Ed was reluctant to dun him. For two weeks or more, he had hardly gone out of the house on his days off.

"Ed, we must do something about Gene."

"We've done it. It's up to him from now on."

"But he's our son."

"God help him."

"Ed! What do you mean by that?"

"What I mean is, he's a man now and I don't think he's going to come to any good, and we can't do a blessed thing about it."

She feared what he said was true, but she wished he had not

put it into words. She cried, and he patted her shoulders. Only, he was so angry and so strong that they were more thumps than pats. To prevent the thumping, she put her arms around him and pressed firmly against him.

On September 1, the radio announced that Germany had invaded Poland and declared war.

"That settles it," Dick cried, and he slapped the checkerboard so hard the pieces scattered.

That morning Gene had phoned in sick, though he wasn't. He was lazy—"bone lazy," as Ed put it—and getting lazier. He was just going to spend the day sitting around and playing checkers.

"What settles what?" he asked.

"I been taking it easy too long," said Dick. "I'm going to ship out tomorrow, if there's a boat. Sis! Hey, Sis! I'm well, I'm going back to sea, you're a great sister, thanks."

"Oh, Dick, are you sure?"

"Yep."

"Why all of a sudden like this?" she asked.

"War."

"It's not our war."

Dick turned to Gene, who for some reason had been staring at him intently.

"One of the things I like best about being a seaman," he said seriously, "is standing watch in the rain. I never have figured out why. I just do. Well, I've been here for two and a half months and it hasn't rained a drop. And here come war clouds, so off I go. What time's the first bus to San Fran in the morning?"

"I'll take you on my bike," said Gene.

"Oh now," said Muriel.

"Don't you work tomorrow?" said Dick.

"Dick," said Gene, and it was the first time Muriel had heard him drop the "Uncle." "Dick, could you get me into the seamen's union?"

Dick shrugged. "I could try. It's a dog's life."

89

"I want to."

"Oh, honey!" She burst into tears. "My baby, what are you going to do?"

"Go to sea. Come on, Mom, if it's all right for Uncle Dick, why isn't it all right for me?"

"That's different," she wailed. "What if there is a war? It's so dangerous. I'll never see you again."

"Oh, Mother, come on." He picked at himself between his legs and shifted in his chair.

"Uncle Sam," Dick drawled, "expects every red-blooded Amurrican to do his duty by his country."

"You're not funny," she said. "You're mean." She felt her emotions starting to give way, and she would have stopped them as she always had done, except for Dick's grin. He was tickled pink with himself; he was mocking her. She let herself go. "You are a mean, wicked man, and I wish Gene had never come under your evil evil influence."

She had never in her life said such a thing out loud to anyone, much less to a member of the family. She ran into the bedroom and threw herself across the bed face down and sidewise. Everything was wrong. Hearing a noise at the door, she reared up, seized by the fright that Dick was coming in to beat her with the baseball bat. It was only the dog. When she had finished sobbing, she did not drop into a restorative sleep or calm down. She breathed irregularly, in spasms, and kept imagining that she was being crept up on, that she was going to be stabbed to death. The radio was on loud. She could hear the voices of Dick and Gene sometimes, but not what they were saying. Neither of them came in to comfort her. They didn't love her.

The back door slammed. Ed had returned from the orchard. The radio clicked off. She heard all three men's voices for a while, then Ed's raised in anger. Then he came into the bedroom and sat on the bed beside her, squeezing her arm with one hand and stroking her hair with the other.

She heard the motorcycle's hroom, the howl of the tires spinning on the dirt, and the roar of the motor dwindling in the distance. Then, the next thing she knew, Ed was no longer there beside her and the sun was in her eyes. She must have fainted. Could a person who was already lying down faint? But you don't just fall into sleep without the least transition. She had never fainted before, though she had sometimes wanted to. Mama said she had fainted as a young woman—and the last year of her life she fainted several times, but that didn't count for she was sick. Muriel struggled up, heavily, and sat on the edge of the bed pulling herself together.

Because Gene and Dick had given her no advance notice, she couldn't make them a good farewell meal, as she ought to. As they ought to have allowed her to. She would have to serve re-heated baked beans, cole slaw with sliced tomatoes, and stewed prunes for dessert. Dick and Ed were talking quietly in the living room as she prepared the food. She listened only for the sound of the returning motorcycle.

They always ate at six. At quarter past, at Ed's insistence, they sat down glumly, just the three of them, and Ed said the long Thanksgiving-and-Christmas blessing. "Amen," Dick said with him, and though Dick went to church no more than Ed, he did not sound ironical when he joined in the amen. Ten minutes later, Gene dashed in, apologized excitedly, gobbled his food— it might as well have been oatmeal for all he noticed—and then announced that he had to run off and tell his buddies good-bye.

Well, at least the merchant marine was not as bad as the army. She remembered how crushed Faith Burger had been the year before when her son up and enlisted. The night he was eigh-teen, two months before graduating from high school, he ran off without a word to his mother, leaving a note for her to find on his pillow in the morning. Faith's only child. Her husband had been in the insane asylum in Napa for years; she had enough money to live without working; no one knew where it came from. She took to her bed, and Muriel, representing the club, vis-ited her every day for a week. "It's like a kick in the abdomen," Faith said. "I gave him everything I could, everything, car, tennis rackets, vacations, spending money. God is my witness, I love him and always did. And this is the reward I get." At least he

91

wrote her a postcard every Sunday, and he had come home on leave for three days at Christmas. Faith seemed back to normal now, and was more active than ever in club affairs. Muriel took heart from this.

She did not believe in the war. Anyhow, President Roosevelt had promised to keep them out of it and she believed he would. Of course President Wilson had been a good man too, for a Democrat, and had promised the same thing. . . .

The next day at one, Gene's boss phoned and asked where he was. At first her heart sank lower yet: he hadn't even made arrangements about the job. She answered in a fading voice. But then the man—Art Sharp, a vulgar Okie with a roll of fat at the base of his neck and acne scars on his pudgy face—began to bawl her out and demand that she pay the balance of what Gene owed on the motorbike, eighteen dollars. That rallied her dignity, and she told *Mister* Sharp in a very formal voice that she would see what her husband had to say about that.

Gene was eighteen years old.

She thought of Father O'Horgan and his *everything has a meaning*. She gave her head a nasty shake. Here Gene owed a dollar for every year he was old, and it didn't mean a thing on earth.

Later that same afternoon, an explosion in the Flattigatti winery—some chemical—injured Al's hunchbacked cousin Mario and set the building on fire so that it was a loss, though many of the vats were saved from destruction. Ed happened to be there at the time, and he was the one who carried Mario out of the burning building. He told her all about it, and she admired him so much that she forgot about Gene for hours. When she did remember, what he had done no longer seemed quite so catastrophic. After all, he might not get into the union; there might not be a job available; if he did ship out, he'd promised to write home right away and she knew he would. She expected to see him back home no later than Sunday, "with his tail between his legs," as Ed put it.

Three days later, Al came by with what at first sounded like

92

good news. He was fully insured against fire, and the chemical company had probably been at fault; the two companies could fight it out between them; meanwhile, he would be getting paid promptly by the insurance people. He'd have to sell this year's crop of grapes to other wineries, and he might have some trouble getting fair compensation for that loss. But all in all, he couldn't complain. In fact, he was glad for the opportunity to expand his winery and change its location to a more advantageous spot.

Then came the bad news, the news that, added to everything else, threw Muriel into the worst tizzy she had ever been in. She could take blows one at a time, but they so often seemed to come at her in clumps.

To show his gratitude to Ed for saving Mario—who would never be the same again though thank God it looked like he was going to pull through—Al was going to build his new winery *here*, on their place, adding onto the barn and having caves dug into the hillside back of it, and he was going to make Ed not only foreman of the new vineyard but assistant manager of the winery and double his salary. Ed would be Al's right-hand man.

Ed was too pleased with this step up in the world for her even to dream of throwing cold water on him for it. And of course it was high time that he was making a decent salary; he had worked hard and honestly all his life, and he deserved it if a man ever did. But to have alcohol being distilled within fifty yards of her own home, and by her own husband! Not even two hundred dollars a month could reconcile her to that.

Two or three times during the discussion, Muriel fanned Al's cigar smoke away from her face. He watched her do this; he had to know how the smoke bothered her. Yet, without the slightest apology, he kept right on emitting clouds of it, not in her direction particularly, just everywhere. What could she do? He was the boss.

Having a bad headache, she ate little for supper that evening, took a double dose of aspirin, and went to bed before it was dark. When the throbbing began to subside, she drowsed, and presently slept.

She awoke to darkness. She did not know where she was, but

93

did not worry about it. Her whole consciousness was filled by Ed's buglelike tenor singing an old hymn they both loved:

> He walks with me and He talks with me
> And He tells me I am His own,
> And the joy we share as we tarry there
> None other has ever known.

When he stopped, she knew where she was and knew he was out of doors in the hot evening. She had not heard him sing like that since the Great War and the Morgan Brothers. The feelings she had known in the *Messiah* chorus when, so long ago, she had first heard his voice ring out had come alive again. As they began to fade in the stillness, she wept for loss.

It was so hot that she had gone to bed without a nightie on, and in her sleep she had kicked the sheet off. There was nothing terrible about sleeping in her birthday suit, and Ed had taken to sleeping in Jenny's old room as soon as Dick left. All the same, he might come in, perhaps to get something from their bureau. Feeling about him as she did now, she was ashamed to have him see her: she was so fat. But, instead of pulling the sheet over her, she lay on her side, not blowing her nose or even wiping her eyes, and she spanked the sack of fat in front of her.

Suddenly, though the room was quite dark and though the ceiling was low, she seemed to see herself from a great height. It was as though she were looking through a telescope: she could see her distant body sharply. There was no bed, no furniture, nothing but her. "Not me, my body. Where am I?" Once she had seen the drawing of a pale foetus, the head huge; only, now, it was her torso that was huge, not the head. She did not want to return into this monstrous body. But the moment she refused to keep on looking at it, she was back in it.

She was afraid she might be losing her mind. She had no one to turn to. She must do something.

Saturday morning, Jenny came home to pack and say goodbye; the next weekend she would be going directly from Santa Rosa to nursing school. She brought the mail in with her.

94

There were a mail order catalogue and a letter from Dunreith, addressed not to them both but to Ed alone, in a handwriting Muriel did not recognize, all capital letters, and with no return address. She tossed them both on the bread box, for the main thing was a postcard from Gene: he was on the same freighter as Dick, headed for Panama. No mention of the motorcycle. Love, Your Son.

"Both my babies deserting me at once!" she wailed, and hid her face in her hands.

"Oh, Mother," said Jenny, giving her a whack on the shoulder and then holding her, "Gene's practically a grown man and he wants to see the world. Is there anything unusual about that? And me, well, for pete's sake, I'm only going to be seventy miles away and we can always talk long distance if we have to. We're not deserting you. We're just growing up, that's all." But then Jenny shed a few tears in sympathy.

She knew exactly how to soften the blow for her mother. She was the best daughter in the world. Muriel wiped her eyes, and Jenny chattered.

By the time Ed came in half an hour later to see if Jenny had got home yet, Muriel was back to normal, putting the finishing touches on Jenny's favorite salad, fruit gelatin with marshmallows and salad dressing. After Ed had hugged Jenny, repeating "Well, honey, well, honey," unsmiling but joyful, he washed up for dinner and then looked at the postcard from Gene.

"The boy got what he wanted. I hope he wants what he's got."

"Oh, Ed, don't you think it's wonderful that he's on the same ship with Dick?"

"We'll know better six months or a year from now, the next time we lay eyes on him."

"Now, Popsy," said Jenny kissing his neck, "don't be glum. Doomsday isn't scheduled for this fall."

"For the year two thousand, to be exact."

"Oh, cripes," Jenny groaned, "gee-muh-nee."

"Do you know what we're having for dinner?" said Muriel holding up a chicken leg dripping batter.

"Southern fried chicken!" squealed Jenny. "My favorite."

95

"And mince pie for Papa."

"How's that, Paw?"

"It's early in the season for mince pie."

"Mary Virginia Jackson gave it to me last Sunday after church. Such a sweet woman. She put it up last year, and she had three pints still on hand and she just wanted me to have one."

"Okay, Papa? Make you feel better?"

He smiled wryly. "Sure, sure." He sat at the table and held one of Jenny's hands in both his. "Well, my dear, so you're going to move to San Francisco next week."

"No!" she said excitedly. "It's all different. I got a special delivery letter Wednesday. I'm accepted at Immaculate Conception in Oakland!"

"For heaven's sake," Muriel said, though she had already heard.

"Why the change?" asked Ed.

"It's one of the two best in Northern California and they are giving me a half scholarship, that's why. Isn't that fabulous?"

"Yes, honey, I'm glad for you," he said. "And don't forget we can help you out financially now, if you need it."

"We're so proud of you," said Muriel.

Jenny laughed.

"Immaculate Conception," said Ed. "Is that what you called it?"

"The Hospital of the Immaculate Conception, and it's run by the Sisters of Mercy."

"That's all right," he said, "but what on earth does the name mean?"

"Now, Papa," said Muriel, "it's just one of those Catholic expressions."

She had wanted to know but had not wanted to ask. The Catholics were strange in so many ways: real wine at Communion instead of unfermented grape juice (of course Episcopalians were that way too), unmarried priests, Latin. And the Virgin; always the Virgin. Why couldn't they just call her Mary, or even St. Mary? But it reassured her so much to think of Jenny's being under the supervision of nuns that she hadn't wanted to ask too

96

many questions, and she didn't want to show that she was glad Ed had asked this one.

"It means," said Jenny, "that St. Anne conceived Mary without original sin. That way, the Blessed Virgin was worthy to be the mother of Jesus."

"Idolatry," said Ed.

"Where did you learn all that?" Muriel asked.

"Eileen Spratt," said Jenny. "She converted this spring."

"Idolatry," Ed repeated.

"It's in the Bible, Papa."

"Is it," he responded flatly. "I know what's in the Bible but I don't believe every syllable of it is true, and I have a pretty good idea of what idolatry is and this is idolatry."

"All right, but that doesn't keep the Sisters from being good nurses, does it?"

"Just so long as you don't convert," said Ed.

Jenny didn't answer right away, and Muriel offered up a silent prayer: "Please, Lord, let this day not be spoiled by family strife."

"I don't plan to," Jenny said in a small voice, "but I do like Eileen, she's my best friend, and I went to Mass with her at Easter."

Ed gazed at her solemnly for a moment. Then his whole face lightened, and he released her hand and patted it.

"Do what's right, my dear. Who am I to tell you what way you should take, when I'm not sure of my own? God bless you, you're a good woman."

"Thank you, Lord," Muriel murmured, the sputter of frying covering the sound of her voice.

All three had moist eyes.

The next day, after Jenny had left, Ed wandered out to the barn for a while, then wandered back in and sat at the kitchen table, drumming his fingers. Their Sunday dinner had been even larger than customary because Jenny was about to leave, and neither wanted so much as a dish of applesauce for supper. Sighing, puffing on a cigar, he stumped into his bedroom, and then came

97

back out. "I feel like a sick dog that can't find a comfortable way to lie down. You know how they go round and round, and stay for a while and then go some place else." He turned on the six o'clock news: war and war and war. Looking disgusted, he switched the radio off. He caught sight of the catalogue on the bread box, reached over for it, and began thumbing through it.

He was making Muriel nervous, but she could not reproach him. She wished she could tease him as Jenny did. "Dingdong, dingdong, come on, Bell, have some fun." She just sat at the table working on a crossword puzzle. Rosemary, who did one a day, had sent her a bookful of puzzles as a gift.

"What's this?" Ed held out the letter from Dunreith.

"Oh, heavens, it completely slipped my mind. It just came yesterday. It must have got into the catalogue somehow."

He dry-licked his lips, frowning but not scolding her, and then sliced the envelope open with his pocket knife.

"Who's it from, dear?" She spoke with more interest than she was feeling.

He looked at the signature first. "Smiley."

Smiley was Fran's youngest, a fourteen-year-old boy whom Ed and Muriel had never seen.

"Why, how sweet of him."

Presently his hands thunked down onto the table, and he stared at her so bleakly that her hands fluttered to her mouth.

"It's Fran and Owen. They had a wreck, last Sunday afternoon on their way home from Wichita, visiting their kids. They ran head on into a Greyhound bus. Fran was killed instantly. Owen died that same night. Smiley stayed home with a sore throat or he'd have been with them. They had to have a closed-coffin funeral. Wednesday morning at Calvary. They're laid next to Mother and Dad. It's all over now."

She did not say anything, but reached across the table and enclosed his clasped hands in hers. They stared for a while at their hands.

"Well, wife, now we're all alone."

She was so shocked by his statement she could not say a

98

word. Alone! Children, friends, relatives, neighbors, each other!

"We haven't got a single close relation left in Dunreith or Ames. All the years we've lived in this Godforsaken dry valley I've felt gone from home. Mother died. Dad died. One by one, they moved away. Now the last are gone. In a closed coffin."

She suddenly became conscious that his hands had once handled dead bodies. There was something morbid about a man who would voluntarily work for an undertaker, as Ed had done, and be good at it.

"I'll never go back now," he was saying, "as I always promised myself I would. What's the use? There's no home to be gone from."

No home! Where were they this very instant? She took her hands back and stared at him with new eyes.

There could be only one reason for him to utter such terrible falsehoods. Of course he was upset, but grief alone could never account for this. He wanted to hurt her. She had never seen this cruelty in him before. He'd always pulled the wool over her eyes by being so thoughtful-seeming, so reliable.

She watched him get up heavily, and walk out into the orchard.

He was unhappy. She was too, but not *that* unhappy, there was not *that* much to be unhappy about. Anyway, unhappiness is no excuse for hurting somebody else. He wanted to tear her away from her friends and make her suffer more than she was suffering already.

All right, if that's the way the wind was blowing, she knew what she would do: make a life of her own. She did not form a resolution about it. She simply knew that was what she was going to do. Taking a deep breath, she squared her shoulders.

The new life began next morning at 8:30 with a phone call from the club's newest, youngest, jolliest member, Camille Piskor.

"Muriel, I'm resigning."

"You're what?"

"Withdrawing my membership."

"I won't hear of it. Has something happened?"

"Yes. I learned that Laura Freundlich's husband is a member of the Bund."

"The what?"

"Well, Lionel and I are both Polish, and I know Laura isn't German but her husband is, and we learned yesterday at the Polish-American Society dinner who the members of the Bund around here are, and Otto Freundlich is one."

"Oh, Camille, this is absolutely awful. What is the Bund?"

"They support the Nazis. So, you see. Sorry."

Club work, yes. And that very month she got active again in the Daughters of the American Revolution, even though it meant driving clear to Santa Rosa to meetings. Mama had been a stalwart in the D.A.R., and Muriel of course had belonged in Ames; but Santa Rosa had seemed too far to drive. But now the time had come. Civic activities of every sort.

What she hadn't reckoned with was how much the war could intrude. For example, a breezy hi-folks postcard from Gene mailed in Gibraltar and then a letter mailed in Marseilles three days later saying they had seen a German submarine blow up a British tanker the day before and had rescued four sailors.

Then Laura Freundlich—oh, why hadn't she been the one to resign so Camille could have stayed in the club?—Laura began trying to get the membership agitated about letting a Jap be the high school valedictorian next year. Her son was second in the class and the top student was Nobuko Nagatoshi, who never did anything but study, no outside activities, no citizenship, just a grind, whereas *her* son . . . Fortunately, Laura could not drum up much support, and Muriel was firm: if Nobuko had the best record, she should be valedictorian and give the graduation speech, Jap or no Jap.

What did *Japanese* have to do with it anyhow? The Nagatoshis worked harder—Ed had often said so—than anybody else in the whole area, growing vegetables and flowers. Nobuko had no outside activity for the good and sufficient reason that she worked in her family's garden every day after school and all day Saturday and sometimes on Sunday too. The Nagatoshis stayed to themselves. Every time Muriel had gone there to buy something, they were so polite she could never get to know them really. She decided to run for the School Board next spring, to see that nothing like what Laura wanted would ever happen.

She wished she knew some bad Germans, Russians, Italians, Japs, so that she could have the proper feelings about going to war against their nations. But all the ones she had ever known, even the Nagatoshis with their awful accents and their smiling, were more American than anything else. Whatever "American" meant really. But if a D.A.R. didn't know the answer to that question, who did? And that slogan that kept popping up these days, "America First"—of course! But why would anybody bother to say it? *For Americans*, it was too obvious to need to be said. "Germany First" *for Germans*, and so on and so on. The Communists were probably to blame for a great deal; everyone said so, like J. Edgar Hoover; they were godless and international and subversive; but it had never become entirely clear to her what they did or how they did it.

She kept trying not to think about politics, but every so often she had to. Ed didn't help matters, listening to the news twice a day and buying the Sunday paper every week. It was the Hearst paper, and of course Hearst was very patriotic; but she hated to have those scandalous articles and photographs sprawled all over her living room every Sabbath. She even caught herself once reading about a starlet who had wrapped her newborn illegitimate baby in newspaper and put him in the garbage can to die; a Mexican cleaning woman, mother of five, had seen her acting suspiciously, looked in the garbage can, fished out the baby, and taken him home to raise as her own; six weeks later, the starlet, remorseful, had kidnapped the baby back; the Mexican woman went to the police about it, and that is how the whole sordid, squalid, wicked wicked mess got into the papers. Hollywood.

When they were first married, they had occasionally gone to moving pictures, but Ed had never seen a talkie. Muriel had gone to a few, mostly with club friends, but of course movies were nearly all as immoral as the actors themselves; also, they were terribly vivid. She felt no great temptation to go, since the nearest theater was in Santa Rosa. That winter, however, the American Legion Post in Montezuma showed a movie every Saturday night in their hall, at the far edge of town, and Al Flattigatti, who was a past commander of the post, insisted on taking Ed and Muriel, as his guests. They ran out of excuses and finally had to go. It was a war movie: tanks, men marching with stiff legs, explosions, machine-gun fire, terrified women and children, planes. The noise was too loud, and the screen had a ripple in it. The movie ended with a picture of the American flag waving against a sky with light summer clouds drifting across and an ominous, solemn voice reciting George Washington's words about entangling alliances.

Ed was all but rude to Al about the movie. "Makes my ears ring. Too darned much racket. If they want to make another war, I can read about it in the paper. I don't have to watch them doing it. Gave me a headache." Al was obviously peeved at Ed, but Muriel was proud of her husband for being so forthright and outspoken to his boss.

It was not till dawn, when a sudden windburst of rain startled her out of sleep, that she realized how much that movie had upset her. She had of course occasionally seen planes flying overhead (though never a warplane that she knew of) and had even seen some quite close up, parked on the other side of a fence in an airfield; she only knew two people who had ever taken trips by plane, though several had gone up for joyrides to see what flying was like. Birds were the most beautiful and wondrous of God's creatures; nothing in all nature gave her more of a thrill than birds; and the sky was for them. She had heard about bombers, but she had never really believed anything that wrong could be, until, clutching onto Ed's arm, there in the American Legion Hall, she saw them committing their evil deeds.

Lying on her side, listening to the rain drumming on the roof, she could not stop the images of the bombers from swelling and swooping and burning in her mind, birds in flight laying monstrous eggs, men operating machines to kill defenseless women and children. Yet the images were somehow remote; silent; beyond her grasp or belief. Yet there they were, vivid, interminable.

Her emotions broke out into the open, free of these images,

102

only when it suddenly occurred to her again that she might be going out of her mind. She had to do something. She must do whatever she could to keep the world from going out of *its* mind too. That very day, she would go down and register to vote, for the first time in her life. That certainly was not enough; still, it was a beginning, though she did not know what it was a beginning to.

She rested much more than formerly. Dr. Baum—she had gone back to him, in spite of his unkindness, because he was so much the best—advised her to rest, but she was careful to see that none of her activities suffered. She continued to be troubled about what to do.

Then one Tuesday in February, by chance, while playing bridge, she got considerable relief. It was her turn to have the bridge club, eight women in all, and though she had warned them about the construction on the barn, they pooh-poohed her and jokingly said she couldn't get out of it that easily.

For weeks, tractors and trucks and strange men and machines had been rumbling past the house, tearing up the orchard, working on the barn. Ed had mentioned, at supper the evening before, that they'd hit granite sooner than they'd expected, excavating in the hillside.

That Tuesday, the bridge party was about to start when a workman came to the back door asking for a bandage; he had a gash on his forearm, and of course Muriel cleaned and bandaged it for him. No sooner were the ladies seated a second time and the cards dealt than a strange-looking gray truck slowly ground its way by the house, with a long crane stretched out in front, nodding and swaying with majestic dignity.

"Never a dull moment," said Faith Burger.

They laughed and settled in to play. But neither table had finished the first rubber yet, when a loud, muffled explosion shook the whole house, making the dishes rattle and dance on their shelves.

"Jesus Christ," said Mary Virginia. She was the minister's wife, and none of them had ever heard her swear before; she did

103

not bat an eye but went right on. "Muriel, this is a battlefield. You're being invaded."

Of course! That was it! For some reason, what Mary Virginia said made her feel much less disturbed, from then on, about both herself and the war. Germany invaded Poland and Czechoslovakia, Russia invaded Poland and Finland, Japan invaded China or someplace over there. It was awful, but it was what was happening everywhere. In June when Germany overran France and the Low Countries, and Italy sneaked into France at the last minute, she felt, powerfully, a confirmation which did not disturb her but gave her strength—though *what* had been confirmed, she did not ask herself.

Late in the afternoon on the Sunday after France fell, when Ed had gone over to Al's to discuss something and she was alone, she went out into the barn and looked around. She had not been in it since Gene went away. There were barrels and vats; no bottles; but lots of pipes and tubes and pumps. It was no longer a barn at all. What was it? She shivered to think of dark caves lurking behind it.

She was invaded all right. Things were beginning to fit together in her mind, not in the old way.

The night after Gene's two-day visit in August, Muriel cried herself to sleep, less from grief at his leaving than from disappointment and dismay at his behavior while he had been with them. He was lean and tan; he swaggered when he walked; he had a new, tight-lipped way of talking; he laughed too much, in Dick's manner; he spent both evenings away from home with his buddies; he never mentioned the eighteen dollars Ed had paid on his motorcycle, and of course Ed was too considerate to bring the subject up first. He had an anchor tattooed on one arm and a lovers' knot with ROSE on the other; when Muriel asked him who Rose was, he burst out singing, "In Dublin, fair city, where the girls are so pretty." At home alone with them, especially at the dinner table, he seemed his old self, affectionate, considerate, interested in what they said; he told them about the serious books he had been reading, history and philosophy mostly but also psychology, and though a lot of it was over his head he liked it better than just playing cards on his time off. Yet, in front of Goodman's when he was leaving, his manner was offhand and jaunty; he told them to say hello Jenny for him, sorry he'd missed her, shook his father's hand and pecked a kiss on his mother's cheek, climbed on the bus, and was gone, grinning through the window at them—"cool as a cucumber," Ed said.

In the dark of the night, cried empty, Muriel woke up with a strange, remote urge to look up Theda Barry. Theda had been in her dream, somehow, beckoning, though to whom or why or for what was unclear. It made no sense for Muriel to see the girl, to whom she hadn't given a thought in a year, but she trusted her impulse. "Thou shalt feel what thou shouldst feel." Well, she felt *this* impulse very strongly, so she should and would act on it first thing in the morning.

The diner was exactly as she remembered it, except that at the end away from the jukebox there was a playpen with a round-headed baby sitting in it, wearing nothing but diapers, waving a rattle. Muriel ordered iced tea, then approached the playpen quietly.

"What an adorable child. The bluest eyes I ever did see."

The woman at the counter showed signs of life. "I've got her for two more days."

"Oh, she's not yours?"

"My daughter's."

"Theda?" The woman nodded. Muriel beamed. "Then you must be Mrs. Barry."

"That's right. How come you know Theda?"

"She was in the senior class play last year, with my son Gene."

"Is that a fact?" Mrs. Barry squinted and leaned forward. "Gene Bell."

"Did you ever meet him?"

Mrs. Barry snorted and drew herself a glass of orangeade.

"Where's Theda now?" said Muriel. "I hadn't heard she was married."

"She's on her honeymoon. They left yesterday."

"Oh, really, yes, I see. Well. Where are they spending it?"

"Stowes Landing. Cabot fishes."

"Cabot Fisher? Is he from around here?"

"Cabot Findlay. He likes to go fishing."

The baby was at the side of the crib making friends with Muriel.

"May I?" said Muriel, picking her up.

"Her name's Shirley Ann."

"Well, Shirley Ann," Muriel cooed as she settled her onto her lap, "Now you've got a father, too."

For some reason this made Mrs. Barry laugh hard and long. Then, as though Muriel had passed some test, had been accepted into some sort of secret society, she told Muriel a great deal about Theda.

She had met Cabot at a dance in Ukiah three weeks before. He had been working as a lumberjack in the woods west of the Eel River, and now he was ready to settle down, if he could just find a job he liked. He was crazy about Shirley Ann, and Theda was crazy about him. He was twenty-five years old and an even six foot tall. He was half-Indian, the same as Theda.

Muriel was sorry she had got Mrs. Barry started, for the longer she went on and the better she tried to make Theda and her marriage sound, the worse it seemed to Muriel. "Like calleth unto like." But the baby was affectionate, blonde, bouncy, gurgling with good spirits. It had been altogether too long since she had played with a baby this way.

"Oh, you're the cuddliest little curlilocks in the whole world. I wish I had a baby granddaughter of my own, just like you."

Mrs. Barry's gum popped.

Muriel froze, staring, holding Shirley Ann at arm's length. "Who is the father?"

"Theda never told."

"How old is she?"

"Five months."

Muriel put her back in the pen as carefully as though she were made of thin glass, picked up her purse, said Good-bye, and headed for the door.

106

"Hey, Mrs. Bell, you forgot to pay."

Muriel paid, then left. She never drove past that diner again if she could help it, and she put Shirley Ann and Theda out of her thoughts firmly and permanently.

Finally, on Thanksgiving Day, Providence brought things together in such a way that she realized what would be the center of her life from then on. She did not make a resolution about it or figure it out; it just came upon her, to her enormous relief.

The week before, Laura Freundlich had been crippled for life in a collision. Otto had been driving under the influence. He had taken a curve too fast, and the car had skidded on the gravel and crashed broadside into a telephone pole. He escaped with minor bruises.

Muriel's first thought, after the shock of hearing this, was: At least he'll have to spend the rest of his life taking care of her. There is some justice. Her second thought was: Now Camille can rejoin the club. She is *so* nice. When Muriel had time to think about these reactions of hers, she was distressed to realize how uncharitable she had been. She resolved to make up for her bad thoughts by going to see Laura at least three days a week so long as she was confined in the hospital and to do what she could for her after she came home. That way, Muriel would kill two birds with one stone: she would give poor Laura a little cheer in a bleak life, and her very presence would keep fresh in Otto's mind what he had done, for Muriel's views on alcohol were no secret.

Jenny was not free to come home for Thanksgiving but had to be on duty at irregular hours all four days of the holiday. Not to see her this time—and she had come home very seldom since she had been going to nursing school—was too much for Ed. *He* suggested that they drive down to Oakland and have Thanksgiving dinner with her in a restaurant. He detested restaurants and hated trips even more, but he, like Muriel herself, would not do without Jenny for too long at a stretch if he could help it. Delighted, Muriel proposed that they take the ferry, for though it was longer than going by the Golden Gate and Bay bridges, it would mean much less city traffic for them. Ed agreed—

107

anything to avoid cities. Her real reason was that she had not been on a ferry, on any sort of ship, for over ten years, the last time she had gone to San Francisco, and she wanted to get a feeling of what Gene liked about sailing; also, she would rather look at the bridges than ride on them.

They got on the ferry near San Quentin penitentiary, and that seemed ominous, though nothing untoward happened. They got off it on Point Richmond, and drove right alongside the huge Standard Oil refinery there. They had never seen one before: pipes, tanks, pumps, stink.

"What is this," said Ed, "hell?"

"Now, Papa," she said, but without much reproach in her voice. It looked like a glimpse of hell to her too.

Jenny was on duty till six, and they got to her dormitory before five. Ed suggested they stretch their legs, and Muriel was curious to inspect the neighborhood.

The nurses' dormitory was across a busy thoroughfare from the hospital itself. They strolled down the sidewalk on the dormitory side. Not three blocks away they came on a bar named Nothing But, the front of it done up to resemble a saloon in the days of gold mining. A slatternly white woman staggered out sidewise through the swinging doors, nearly bumping into them, cursing under her breath. Teetering on the curb, she swung her purse vaguely but viciously in the direction of the Nothing But. A Negro man with bloodshot eyes came out, walked over to her slowly but without swaying or stumbling, took her by the arm firmly, and, speaking to her soothingly in a bass mumble, led her away.

"Disgusting," Muriel said. Ed spat and wiped his chin. "To think," she went on, "that Jenny is exposed to this every day of her life."

They were in the lobby when Jenny burst in, glowing, happy to see them. After the hugs and hellos, Jenny introduced a swarthy, skinny, shy little girl as her "pal" Carry Nation Furbelow, who was all alone that evening because her family lived in Copperopolis, way past Stockton, and her boyfriend, an ambulance driver, was on duty till midnight. Of course they invited

Carry to join them for dinner. Muriel was relieved that Ed kept his annoyance from showing but let his good feelings at being with Jenny spill over onto her pal. Carry was friendly enough, smiling appreciatively, and she had the good manners not to join in the conversation with more than a word here and there. Muriel regaled them with her story about the real Carry Nation, whom she had gone to hear address a temperance meeting in Wichita when she was attending Miss Turner's School for Young Ladies. She told them how impressive it was to see her flourish the very hatchet with which she had smashed hundreds of bottles of liquor in saloons.

As they were driving back toward Richmond to catch the 9:30 ferry, it was drizzling and blowy. They were driving at thirty-five miles per hour, the speed limit, since Ed was worried about being on time and there was not much traffic; also, he seemed always to drive at that speed around Twin Creek Valley, on curves, on the paved road, even through rural intersections; he hated automobiles, gripping the wheel as though he expected the car to buck on him at any moment.

A youth on a motorcycle—it might have been Gene— roared past them, his wheels between the streetcar tracks, and then cut in front of them. But, as he swerved, his wheels caught in the tracks, and the machine slid out flat, wheels first, and he was thrown free. He skidded on his back, feet foremost, for what seemed to be half a block. The machine came to a stop on its side in the middle of the next intersection. They stopped to see what they could do. The youth had got onto his feet before they could reach him. He shook his head groggily and the heels of his hands were bleeding, but he rudely rejected Ed's offer of help; he reeled over to the motorcycle and yanked it upright; it was dripping oil; he could not start it. He cursed, and let them drive him to a service station several blocks down the street. Muriel thought she detected alcohol on his breath, though she couldn't be positive. At least, as he got out, he said "Thanks"—just before he slammed the door much harder than he needed to.

As they drove off, Ed barked, "Scum."

"He'd probably been drinking," said Muriel.

109

"He's a born fool, that's for sure."

Ed held the steering wheel with straight arms, his knuckles white, and drove on exactly as before.

Muriel could feel her heart palpitating. By the time they reached the refinery her breathing was more or less normal again, but she felt unnaturally alert. The refinery was all lit up. Pumps were going. No one was in sight. Steam was coming out here and there.

Images of pipes dripping colored liquids obsessed her: oil, gasoline, wine.

The ferry rolled heavily, though there did not seem to be much wind. Ed felt queasy and went outside for fresh air. A dozen or so people were sitting about in the large dining room, but they were not making enough racket to disturb her.

The refinery. The winery. The drunk woman in front of the saloon, and her nigger. Laura Freundlich and Otto. Invasions. War. Motorcycles. Civic duty. Carry Nation.

Things were getting out of hand, and alcohol was the worst cause of trouble. Temperance was the only answer. Then Muriel knew: her cause in life from now on would be to make it as hard as possible for people to ruin their lives with drink.

Of course, with Repeal, temperance had received a terrible blow; it was not a popular cause now, and the WCTU no longer had as good a name as it used to. All the more reason for her to join the movement. Not that Ed would like it a bit. She knew a great many women, through PTA, D.A.R., club work, church, and she could find co-workers throughout California. They would have to work quietly, gather their forces behind the scenes, until they were strong—and then strike.

Ed came in. The ferry was about to land. She took a deep breath and smiled at him fondly. He reacted with a little wink and by holding out his arm in a courtly gesture. At their wedding, Dick had said to her when he gave her the kiss of congratulation, "You couldn't have done better, Sis. Ed is one of nature's gentlemen." She recalled this now, and felt a rush of gratitude for Dick's understanding and for Ed's courtesy. She took his arm, giving it a squeeze, and they went down the stairs to their car.

Riding in the night, she thought how sad it was that Dick had been shell-shocked, changing him from the man he might have been. She had intended to tell Ed about her temperance activities right away, but now, somehow, she resolved not to until they were well advanced. Life had given him a lot of hard knocks, too. No use to upset him before she had to.

When Rosemary invited her to join the League of Women Voters, she was glad to, for the purpose of widening the circle of her influence, even though it meant that many more trips to Santa Rosa and even though she had heard some pretty liberal things about the league. For the same purpose, she worked to get elected as a member of the Montezuma School Board and as a vice-president of the California Federation of Women's Clubs, even though this meant at least three trips a year to Sacramento.

It was discouraging to learn how little response temperance elicited among her acquaintance, how low the cause had sunk throughout the state, the nation. In fact, in the entire year until Pearl Harbor, when the movement pretty much suspended activities for the duration of the war, she accomplished little more than to make herself part of the invisible network of women in California who had not given up on temperance. The general drift of opinion seemed to be toward compromise: local option.

A month after Pearl Harbor, Gene enlisted in the Air Force, hoping to become a fighter pilot. He wound up as a bombardier in the European "theatre."

Jenny spent the war as a surgical nurse in a Navy hospital in Hawaii. In more than three years, they saw her only once.

Either Ed or Muriel, sometimes both, wrote to both children every Sunday. They were lucky to get a letter a month in reply.

Ed declared he wouldn't let "this fool war" change his ways and kept right on making wine. Sometimes when the breeze was wrong, the odors from the winery literally made her sick to her stomach. He kept a jug of wine behind the chest in his bedroom.

She didn't know which was worse, Ed's making wine because people wanted it or Gene's dropping bombs on cities because of the war. She had to do something constructive, as Jenny was doing, to make up a little for their activities. Because of the shortage of teachers, she was able to get an emergency credential to teach first grade.

It was tiring work, and many of the children had never been taught manners, much less the alphabet. But most of them were so sweet and so willing to learn that she was happy to have them under her guidance. Even the worst of them were a little less uncouth when they left her room in June than they had been when they had entered it in September. Every year, some of them would make little love-presents for her, usually a crayon drawing which she would tack on the wall. She would cry a little to see them go. The second-grade teacher was perfectly nice, if limited in some ways as old maids are; it was just that Muriel got to love the children and felt a wrenching in her heart each year when they left her. So full of affection and readiness; quivering with eagerness; innocent; but what did life have in store for them? There was so much trouble in the world these days.

Teaching meant a growing savings account, but also that she could not cook noon dinner for Ed on weekdays. Grumbling (but after all, those savings were their only protection against old age), Ed agreed they could have their main meal in the evening, though not on Sundays. Secretly, she was gratified by this partial victory; now they had their "dinner" in the evening like most Californians—even though Ed in his farmerish stubbornness called it "supper" still and would not permit her to use the right name for it in his presence. She encouraged him to read aloud to her for half an hour or so as she was preparing the food. He read *Paradise Lost* and *Paradise Regained* through; even though they both had trouble understanding the poetry, they enjoyed its uplifting qualities. And Ed read very well, inspiringly, especially *Pilgrim's Progress*, when he got to it. The thought occurred to her that it might have been better for him if he had become a missionary as he had originally intended. Of course, in that case, they would never have met. . . . But then he read *David Copperfield* nearly as well as the others, and that was a consolation to

112

her. She felt more at home with Dickens than with any other writer.

Gene was discharged in 1944 and made it home early Christmas Day. That dusk, still logy from the huge dinner, they were sitting in the living room chatting. Ed and Gene were openly drinking wine; granted the occasion, she could not bring herself to mar their fun. Gene seemed so strange to her that she said very little, but Ed was easy with him.

"No," said Gene, "I lost my nerve."

"Well, that sounds funny, my boy," said Ed. "You put in your full share of missions."

"Plus an extra. And that's what did it. Flak."

"Flak?"

"A piece of it through my buddy's Adam's apple, right there on the bench across from me. Over Hamburg. So, as soon as we got back, I had myself grounded."

"You confessed your fear. That's not the same as losing your nerve."

"You sound like a psychiatrist."

"God forbid."

"They send you to one when you ground yourself. Mine just talked with me for a quarter of an hour or so. He said it was good sense for me to be afraid and good sense to admit it, and there was nothing to worry about." She noticed that Gene's laugh was, like Dick's, buffoonish. Why? "So I went out and tied one on. Man, it's really something when you get patted on the back for losing your nerve."

"You're being too hard on yourself."

"No. Dick's the hero, and one hero per family is enough."

"Dick?" said Muriel.

"Sure. You know he's been on two ships that went down?"

Muriel's breath sucked in, and her hands flew to her ears.

"I take it he's all right now," said Ed in a calm voice. "We haven't seen him but once since the war started, and that for just a couple of days. He never writes."

113

"Once his ship hit a mine off the coast of Ireland and he was one of five survivors. The other time they got dive-bombed in the Channel, and the ship broke apart that night. Everybody was saved. He shipped right back out two days later, for Halifax. Me, I not only won't fly anymore, I won't even sail in the merchant marine."

"You can't be blamed for that," said Ed.

"And you must not blame yourself," said Muriel.

Gene laughed. "Easier said than done."

Sometime later in the evening, Ed asked him what he had it in mind to do.

"Get me a job."

"War work?"

"Not necessarily. I thought maybe I'd just lay around home here for a while. If you don't mind."

"Oh, honey," said his mother, "mind?"

"I've taken to reading a good deal, and the more I read the less I understand why this war ever got started. Maybe I'll never understand it, but I'm going to try. I liked those bombsights I had to work. I've been thinking I might try to get me a job in some optical firm, maybe, making precision instruments. Microscopes maybe. You need training though."

He scarcely left the house for ten days. All his former buddies were in the service. He ate a lot, and appreciatively. He was subdued, quiet, friendly with his parents. But he seemed jittery and smoked too much. He seemed always to have something on his mind.

After he had gone off to San Francisco to look for a job, Ed declared himself pleased with the changes in him—all for the better. Muriel agreed warmly, but she also wondered to herself what Gene's secret could be. He had one.

Eight months and nothing much else later, one morning as she was eating her breakfast, coffee and toast with grape jelly, she tuned into the eight o'clock news report and learned about Hiroshima. She debated whether to go looking for Ed, who was already out working, probably in the vineyard somewhere, and tell

114

him what had happened. The end of the war, yes, but such a bomb. She decided there was no point in upsetting him before she had to. Besides, he might very well have heard it on the radio already and not told her so as not to upset *her* so early in the morning. But no sooner had this idea occurred to her than she rejected it. He would have woken her, all right; he relished doom. Her mouth twitched. She was going to spare him anyway.

Within an hour she phoned in her resignation from her teaching job, and by five that afternoon she had written and mailed twenty-five letters to temperance women. "Having won the war, we must not lose the peace. We must not let the multitude of new problems in the world blind us to the age-old evil of alcohol."

By another of those coincidences that keep life interesting, Jenny was due home on leave the very next week. As it happened, her plane got to San Francisco the day following V-J day, and when she finally reached Montezuma by bus she brought horrifying stories about the mob craziness taking place on blocks and blocks of Market Street all day and all night and that very minute still, looting, rape, drunkenness, who could say what all. It was in *The Examiner* next day, too. Muriel would have put it out of her mind except that it kept coming back through conversations. Therefore, she converted the rioting into striking evidence of the consequences of drinking. As Father O'Horgan had pointed out, disturbing images are much more manageable when you know what they mean.

Jenny was the same as ever—of course! A little heftier, but cheery and warmhearted. She had given up smoking, but she drank beer in front of her mother. Also, Muriel remained troubled by the glint in her eye when she was telling about the rioting in San Francisco. If Jenny had a weakness it was her love of fun—anything for a "fun time." But this disgusting *orgy* on Market Street was the furthest thing from fun; fun is healthy. Yet, "awful," said Jenny's voice; "fascinating," said her eyes.

The next day Gene arrived with more stories of the mob violence. His words were more neutral than Jenny's had been, but his eyes looked brooding, gloomy, full of hatred. At one point she heard him saying, "When I saw him do that" (Muriel had not noticed what the *that* was and did not ask), "I could have killed him." "Oh, honey," she said, "you don't mean what you said. Say you didn't mean it." "Yeah," he mumbled, "well, okay."

Muriel thought: My husband and both my children not only drink, they have so little respect for my feelings that they drink in front of me. At first, she wanted to make an issue of it, but she simply could not spoil this family reunion, the first in so long—not after all the years of the heartsickness of never being sure: *Is he all right? Where is he now? When will they come home?* No, she must just rise above the pain their drinking caused her. She decided she would wait till the children had departed, then move Ed's drinking jug back into his bedroom and make him do it in there or out in the winery itself—not in her kitchen and living room at the very least.

Meanwhile, she would tell none of them about her temperance work. Everybody has a little secret, and she had hers. She would spring her surprise on them when she had to, but not before.

Gene had gotten a job with an optical company, all right, and he liked the work. But he was too restless. As he told his parents, he had to "keep moving." Before the end of August, he had a position with the State Highway Patrol.

Gene a policeman! She would never have believed it. She hoped he would stick with this job. Maybe it would have a steadying influence on him. She said she was sorry they were stationing him way down in Fresno; but really she wasn't, for the distance meant she would not know enough about what he was doing to worry about him too much. He was a man now, on his own; she did not want her energies to be distracted from the cause any longer.

When Jenny was transferred to a naval hospital in San Diego that winter, one more burden—albeit a light one—was lifted from Muriel's shoulders. The four people in the world who mattered most were in the same state, but not too close together. Once the children got married and settled down, she would be completely free for temperance.

In January they got a long distance phone call from Dick. He was fine, he hoped they were all fine, he was visiting Jenny in San Diego, he would be shipping out again soon, he didn't know when he would get to see them next.

Ed's work went its own way. She never asked about it. He was busier than ever, and so was she. They had enough money.

She was working for temperance almost literally night and day. The movement was beginning to pick up a gratifying amount of support. They fully expected to get Local Option on the ballot two years from now, in 1948.

As they were finishing dinner on the evening of June 18, the phone rang, and, since it was usually for Muriel, she answered.

"Hi, Mom."

"Genie! How wonderful to hear your voice."

"Guess where I'm calling from."

"Not Fresno or you wouldn't ask."

"You'll never guess."

"Tell me, honey."

"Reno."

"Reno, Nevada?"

"What other Reno is there?"

Ed mouthed *Reno?* at her. When she nodded and shrugged, he ran his tongue around his gums.

"What are you doing in Reno? Not gambling, I hope."

"Nothing like that. Just a few slot machines. Mom, you remember Theda in that senior class play?"

"Theda Barry."

"Yes, only she got married to a guy named Findlay. Well, she's here for a divorce. He wants it, too, because he's going to stay in Japan, he's in the Air Force. So anyway this is like a celebration, sort of, because it was eight years ago tonight that we were in *A Thief There Was.*"

"Yes? Doesn't she have a child?"

"Shirley Ann's the cutest, smartest, sharpest little tyke you ever saw. She's right here in the room now."

"I saw her as a baby."

"You did! Where?"

117

"I happened to drop by Mrs. Barry's diner. Theda was off on her honeymoon."

"Yes, well, then you understand all about Shirley Ann and everything."

"Why are you phoning, Eugene?"

"Gosh, Mom, you don't have to bite my head off. We just got married this afternoon."

Muriel turned from the mouthpiece and spoke to Ed in a light voice which her own ears heard as false. "Gene married Theda Barry this afternoon in Reno."

"Mom? Mom? Were you telling Pop? Can I speak to him? Mom?"

She watched Ed push himself up and stamp on heavy heels. Only after he had banged the door behind him, did she turn back to the phone.

"He just went outside."

"Well, call him, can't you?"

"I'll try."

"I really want to say hello to him."

She called loud enough for Gene to know she had tried but not loud enough for Ed to hear her. She was afraid to put him on the phone; he might say something to Gene so undiplomatic that it could not be taken back.

"I'm sorry, honey. He must be out in the barn."

"We were planning to drive down tomorrow so everybody could get to know each other, but if Pop is going to act this way, I don't know."

"You didn't tell us ahead of time, Gene."

"We didn't tell Theda's mother either. Under the circumstances. Also, her father disappeared years ago. We thought it might as well be a surprise."

"Please come as soon as you can get here. That will be something anyway."

"You don't have to look at it that way."

Tears were streaming down her cheeks. She felt she could not restrain the sobs much longer.

"Good-bye, honey. Tomorrow."

Too heavy to get up, she sat there for half an hour waiting for Ed to come back to her. He did not. The weeping did not last long. She sat picking at a rent in her apron, unable to keep hold of a thought. It seemed to her that if she did not talk with someone, immediately, she would die.

She rang the McPhersons' number; no answer. There was no one else she could turn to, now, but Jenny. She wished Rosemary had been home so she could talk herself out with her best and oldest friend first. Then she would have regained enough equilibrium, maybe, to go over it with her daughter. She resolutely did not consider what she would do if Jenny were not home. "Sufficient unto the day is the evil thereof."

Jenny answered on the first ring.

"Mother! What's the matter?"

"Gene just called."

"Well, golly, did he have an accident? Is he all right?"

"He is in Reno."

"Oh?" Jenny's voice became cautious, unsurprised. "What's he doing there?"

"He got married this afternoon."

"Really?" Jenny's enthusiasm rang false. "Who to?"

"Jenny, you knew all about it, didn't you?"

"Theda? Is it Theda?"

"You knew."

"Remember, I went up to Fresno for that weekend in March? Well, Gene was already seeing Theda a lot. You know. She and her mother moved there during the war. They were running a pet shop, and he just happened to go in."

"Oh sure."

"Honestly. He was going to buy a guinea pig to give to his landlady's little boy for a birthday present. Mother?"

"Go on."

"Well, anyway, he said that they were thinking about getting married, but I haven't heard anything definite."

"You didn't tell me."

"Mother, *Gene* didn't tell you."

"Nobody told me."

119

"She had to get a divorce. He didn't think you'd approve."

"Didn't *think!*"

"He didn't want to upset you any sooner than necessary."

"So," said Muriel with all bitterness, "he waits till he can throw a Digger Indian's bastard in my face instead."

"Mother!" Shock made Jenny's voice genuine. "Where's Pop?"

"You know what he does on occasions like this. He goes outside and communes with nature half the night. Leaving me by myself."

"I never heard you like this before."

"You never had reason to, and neither did I."

"You know about Theda's daughter, don't you?"

"No thanks to you *or* Gene, yes, I do. I saw her before she could walk."

"You know who her father is?"

"Theda didn't tell her own mother who he was, and I don't want to know."

"Gene."

"I said I didn't want to know."

"Mother, listen, Gene is the father of Shirley Ann. She is your grandchild."

"You're lying. Why are you lying to me?"

"You remember how strange he acted that summer? Why do you think he ran off to sea all of a sudden like that?"

"Jane Hypatia, how long have you been keeping this from me?"

"Mother! Are you all right? Is Papa around? Your voice sounds strange. Are you all right?"

"No, I am not all right, and neither are you."

"Mother, you . . ."

"I am going to hang up now."

She stared at the phone with hollow loathing. It rang many times, stopped, rang many more times. What she had just learned meant nothing. The telephone had plastered the life out of it. A corpse of meaning. Even a letter would have been alive to hold. Baring her clenched teeth, she sprayed a little spit on the phone.

Plasterer! Turns everything into information. She studied it as it rang eighteen times. When it stopped, she took the receiver off the hook and let it dangle.

She dragged her fat to bed. Men in her head beat her with clubs till she passed out.

A man shook her awake. "Muriel." She stared at him without knowing who he was. "Wife." It was all right then. "Hello, wife."

"Yes?"

She remembered what had happened and what was about to happen. She told him.

His reaction was not what she was prepared for. Instead of uttering some rude oaths and stamping out, he sat by her and took her hand. He said words she did not understand. What got through to her was the concern in his voice. She gave way.

Sometime later—how long?—she started up. He was still sitting there, touching her.

"Ed? You must go to bed, dear. It's so late."

"Ssh." He pressed her brow with his rough hand, and she sank back onto the pillow. "Sleep, my dear. You are having bad dreams, but sleep."

"Did I talk in my sleep?"

"Yes. I couldn't make any sense out of it. No matter. Go back to sleep. Your soul needs to rest."

Again she came to in the dark. He was not there.

"Ed?" she whimpered. "Where are you, Ed?"

He was beside her in no time.

"I was just pouring myself a cup of coffee out of the percolator. Would you care for some?"

"Our granddaughter. Our only grandchild."

"They'll be here tomorrow. At least we'll get to see what she looks like."

"Do you suppose he really . . ."

"Ssh. Go to sleep. We'll talk another time."

"Bridesmaid at her own parents' wedding. Not that they had a bridesmaid." She howled like a dog.

With both hands, Ed held her head from tossing, till she gave way again and slumped back to sleep.

But by noon she had pulled herself together enough to function, and it was Ed who was down—with a sick headache, the first since her father had pulled all of Ed's teeth, the year before Jenny was born.

Men, she thought. Trust them to run out on a woman every time. Like father, like son.

Children, she thought. "O sharper than a serpent's tooth, a thankless child." What's wrong with Jenny that she hasn't got married yet and given us a proper grandchild?

In her anger, she started to put through a long distance call to San Diego then and there, *collect*, but she remembered that Jenny was on duty till three and hung up on the operator. This anger was the first full, clear emotion she had felt since the call from Gene.

They pulled in at 4:30 and stayed two nights. Muriel did not look Gene in the eye once; when she had to speak to him, she concentrated on a tiny scar just above the bridge of his nose. She gave Theda the Nagatoshi polite treatment; when she told Theda about that visit to the diner (Mrs. Barry had apparently never mentioned it) and how adorable Shirley Ann had been, she absolutely glazed Theda with gush. It was hard to tell much about Shirley Ann except for her eyes. She had been carsick coming through the Sierras, she had a runny nose, she whined, she chewed her thumbnail—and, with her mother's eyes, she watched.

Because of Ed's condition, everybody had to be very quiet in the house. Gene and Theda spent a lot of their time driving around trying to locate old friends to say hello to. They wanted to leave Shirley Ann with her grandmother, and of course Muriel was *dying* to get to know her better, but with Ed feeling so poorly and all it was out of the question.

No one mentioned that Shirley Ann was Gene's real daughter.

No one mentioned it to Muriel again for the rest of her life, except Ed twice and Jenny once. Several times over the years,

122

she had the impulse to object that Shirley Ann should not call him "Gene," in that disgusting modern way, but "Papa" or "Daddy." But how could she broach the subject without raising the other one with it? She let the whole thing slide.

Two springs before, Ed had added a screened arbor onto the north side of the house, and they had trained wisteria to grow over it. By some freak, when people were seated in a certain spot on the far side of the arbor, she could nevertheless distinctly hear what they were saying.

That fall, it appeared in the newspapers that she was one of the moving spirits in the drive to put a Local Option proposition on the state ballot next year, and a couple of days later she was napping in the middle of the afternoon—doctor's orders—when she heard loud voices approach, the scrape of benches or chairs, and then, suddenly clear, Al Flattigatti's voice.

"Well, by God, no wife of mine would ever try a trick like that, and if they did, I know damn well what I'd do to her." He spat noisily.

She could just imagine his putting the dead stump of a cigar back between his fat lips, wallowing it around a time or two, and then clamping the stinking wet thing in his white teeth.

"Now, listen, Al," said Ed.

"I'd take off my belt and beat some sense into her."

She held her breath.

"Well, I'm not going to do anything of the kind to Muriel, is that clear? I don't like what she's up to any better than you do, but she is entitled to her own opinions and that's that."

"If I thought this fool option had a prayer in hell, I'd fire you, Ed Bell, for your wife like that."

"Go ahead, fire me. You can fire me any time you want to. My wife is *my* wife. Fire me."

"I can't, God damn it, you know that. You're my right arm. How can a man fire his right arm?"

"Nothing will come of it."

"Like shit it won't. It's coming of it right this minute. I'm so mad I could chew nails."

"Here's a glass of barbera."

"No. I go home and get drunk on grappa with my *friends*. No horseshit, but plenty of horselaugh. At me."

Scrape of feet, and their angry voices dwindled off into mumble.

When Ed came into the house at five, he said his stomach was sour, he had no appetite for supper. She reached into the oven and triumphantly pulled out a pie.

"Vinegar pie, all for you, honey."

"I thought pies were supposed to be so bad for me you'd never make another."

She put it on top of the refrigerator to cool, then beamed at him. "Don't you want it, Ed?"

"Doggone, if women don't beat the band."

He ate half of it at dinner and the other half for breakfast, to her gratification. She never told him why she had made it, just as he never told her about his argument with Al.

For the year until the election, she cherished the memory of Ed's defense of her, even though it rankled that he was so sure prohibition was dead and gone forever. Then, at the polls, Local Option was thoroughly defeated, and she hardened against him. He had been right, which made it all the worse. Still, he never gloated and he never brought up the subject of her temperance activities.

His attacks of Bright's disease had been getting more frequent over the years, and now Dr. Baum called it chronic. The new miracle drugs didn't seem to work on Ed. She could not get Dr. Baum—the man was stubborn as a mule—to say Ed's kidneys had been weakened by a lifetime of drinking, as they obviously had been.

Wild horses could not have made her quit the temperance movement, what there was left of it, that is; but in fact no one whatever tried to influence her to get out. Therefore, lacking opposition, she had only one reason to continue, hope, and that was in precious short supply. She withdrew passively, by not showing up at meetings, by leaving letters unanswered.

The School Board needed her attention badly. There was a unified district proposal in the offing. Always something.

And bridge. Lots of bridge.

The League of Women Voters could be banked on to have burning issues on hand. She wished she could get more worked up about the league ladies. She agreed with every single one of their principles; they were more American than the flag, practically; she knew perfectly well that there was nothing so precious as our heritage of freedom, but if only the people who were having their rights trampled on weren't such unsavory characters. A criminal syndicalist agitator with an unpronounceable name. A divorced man who murdered his own two children so his wife couldn't have them—was he sane? Had the police used third degree on a Mexican dope addict prostitute? Why was it always the wrong people you had to worry about the rights of? The principle of the thing, that's why of course. Sighing, she resolved to take a more active role in the League.

Who would right her wrongs?

No, she did not have wrongs as the unfortunate did. Yet, she had a sense of terrible wrong. All her life, she had tried to do right, as her mother had gloriously succeeded in doing. She strained with all her might to understand where she had gone wrong, where things had gone wrong; but she could not.

Early in the spring of 1950, Gene was transferred to Santa Rosa, and they settled in a squalid part of town in a rambly, dirty white, stucco, oversized bungalow with a dirt yard. Theda's mother didn't come with them. Theda told Muriel her mother was so attached to the pet shop she couldn't bring herself to leave; but Gene, in the coarsest way, snorted and said she had a boyfriend. Well, Muriel thought, some boy that would be. At least, Theda had the rudiments of respectable manners. She understood about keeping things smoothed over. She could be taught.

The next month, Jenny arrived, her beat-up old La Salle loaded to the gills with her worldly goods. She had left the job completely and was going back to Hawaii for the first time since the war—to see old pals and give herself a good vacation, it was such a fun place, and the climate was heavenly. She had no plans for the future. All she knew was that she'd had enough of

125

Navy hospitals and too much of surgical nursing. She was never going to pass another forceps again in her life. She tried to give them her television set, but Ed wouldn't allow it to be hooked up in *his* house. Not that Muriel particularly minded, for she had not liked the little she had seen of television, but for form's sake she registered her complaint. They stored the set in the shed.

The Sunday before Jenny was to sail, Gene brought his family up to the ranch for dinner. In the middle of the afternoon, Theda and Shirley Ann drove off by themselves; Shirley Ann had never seen the diner or the house where she was born, and Theda thought it was about time. Muriel approved heartily.

She lay down for a little rest.

A door banged, then Gene's low voice came to her—half mumbling as he was doing nowadays, through stiff lips, but still understandable.

"Oh hell. I can't complain about her too much. Her mother's the lollapalooza."

"Well, you left her in Fresno."

"Damn right. You know what happened? Theda's father showed up, after all these years. It turns out her parents never got divorced."

"I can tell you one thing, son, if I ever leave your mother, I'll divorce her and never set eyes on her again for the rest of my natural life."

"Me too, but here comes old Barry and wants to move back in, and her with a boyfriend already. Oh well, what the hell, what's it to me? Live and let live, that's what I say. It got under Theda's skin, though. She's got a will of iron."

"Women do."

The door banged. Jenny's voice joined theirs: "What are you guys talking about?"

"Marriage," said Gene.

"Your mother's a good woman," said Ed, "and she tried hard, but sometimes I wonder how I stood it all these years."

"Theda's no worse than I am," said Gene. "It's marriage."

"Marriage is an invention of the devil," said Ed.

"Now, fellows," said Jenny, "knock it off."

"He's right," said Gene. "Bachelor girl, you're the only smart one in this family."

She laughed raucously. "Come on, Genie, have another great big glass of dago red. You too, Pops. Drown your troubles, boys. Come on, bottoms up."

4

Widow

Only after Ed's dropsy got so bad that he had to be taken to the hospital did Muriel allow herself to admit how tired she felt every morning and how often she had trouble focusing her eyes.

The right medicines had been wrong for Ed all the way, and there were "renal complications." She no longer tried very hard to keep up with all the new medical terms: allergy, antibiotics, nephritis (which was Bright's disease only different), functional disorders, a hundred more, and a new one every time she opened a magazine.

Thank the Lord, all the men working for the Twin Creek Winery had medical and hospital insurance. Otherwise Ed would have had to go into the county hospital instead of the Good Shepherd in Santa Clara—such a superior hospital. She had to take back all the bad thoughts about Al Flattigatti that had fumed up in her during the Local Option campaign, because during Ed's long-drawn-out illness Al was the soul of thoughtfulness with her. So far from putting pressure on her about the house, he offered financial assistance if she needed it; thank heaven, she didn't, but the offer was a real support to her spirits in a tragic time. He was even considerate enough to throw away the cigar stub before he came into the house to make the offer.

People were so good to her. Rosemary insisted she stay in their spare bedroom while Ed was in the hospital. "Till he's back on his feet"—though everybody knew his condition was really serious; Dr. Baum was not one to mince words.

Now, her only occupation, really, was visiting Ed. Rosemary, at Muriel's own request, kept her on a strict diet, though she usually sneaked in a couple of doughnuts a day with her coffee in the hospital cafeteria. Dr. Baum had been downright brutal with her the last time she had gone to him for a checkup: "You are eating yourself into an early grave." What a vulgar, cheap, crude way to put it. Still, he was right about the advisability of her losing. "You know my receptionist?" he said. "Well, she's about your height, and she weighs about what you ought to. Now suppose she had a hundred-and-fifty-pound sack of cement tied on her shoulders. She wouldn't be able to get out of her chair. You're an amazing woman, Muriel Bell; you're stronger than most men. But it can't go on any longer." And he used another jawbreaker to scare her with, arteriosclerosis. While she was still in his office, she was properly impressed, but when she had the door safely shut behind her, she sniffed. She had a right to be tired and draggy; she had been under strain for a long time. After a month at the McPhersons', she was happy to discover that she had lost five pounds.

But her eyes; she had to do something about them. She didn't dare ask Dr. Baum to recommend an eye doctor. The only one she had ever gone to, back during the war when she was teaching, had pried and spied into her pupils in the most horrible way, and then all he had come up with was a weak pair of glasses she only used when her eyes got too tired. Now, she just needed new glasses; she looked in the telephone directory and picked a name she liked, A. J. Bernard, Optometrist.

Lo and behold, *Dr.* Bernard turned out to be a girl. A lanky, rawboned girl in a white smock and flat shoes, with bushy brown eyebrows that grew together in the oddest way and a tough New York way of talking. Optometrists fitted you to glasses; they weren't supposed to peer into your eyes so much—as though they were trying to locate *you*—but this one did. "Muriel," she said—and that was to Muriel the crowning insult, that she had to say *Dr.* Bernard while being called *Muriel* by this whippersnapper (whippersnapper was for boys but A. J. Bernard was a whippersnapper nonetheless)—"Muriel, you must go see your regular physician immediately. I can prescribe lenses that will give you some relief, but there are complications which . . ." Oh, of course, complications; you could always bank on complications.

Jenny was with her the last ten days. She was a special duty nurse at a sanatorium above Honolulu where alcoholics went to get cured; she had accumulated quite a lot of vacation time, and of course she would stay just as long as her mother needed her. They moved back home, for their own sakes as well as for Rosemary's. Jenny wanted to take care of Ed at home, but Dr. Baum thought it would not be advisable.

Ed passed on at three in the morning—the worst hour of the twenty-four, as he'd used to say. Jenny was by his side, holding his hand, at the moment of passing.

Muriel was home in bed at the time, exhausted. Not exhausted: turned to lead. She had known that the end was near, but she had let Jenny persuade her to stay home and try to sleep.

The truce in Korea had been signed the day before. Ed's life was over at the same time the war in Korea was over. There those two big facts stood staring at her; but they would not connect. Besides, the cause of the Korean war was not solved at all. Those Communists, why didn't they stay in their own country and leave other people in peace? It had been so much nicer in the old days. These terrible wars they were having: radar, nuclear weapons, mustard gas, bacteriological warfare, missiles. Could anybody understand it? No one she knew even pretended to.

Leaden. In and out of sleep all night, till Jenny came home from the hospital.

Where was Dick? Almost a month before, Gene had discovered the destination of the ship he was on, Tokyo, and sent him a cablegram. Ten days ago, they had got an airmail letter from him promising to be there. Then, not another word. She tried to get Gene to follow up again, through the union maybe, but he refused. He said Dick ought to know what he was doing.

Smiley would be at the funeral. He had moved from Kansas to California after the war and settled down in San Jose. He was a foreman in an automobile assembly plant, and he had a wife and three children, a girl and twin boys. Somehow, they had managed to get together with him only twice, years before, but over the phone he promised Muriel to come up to Santa Rosa to the funeral. The only other member of the family from either side to be there.

Numb, she left everything to Jenny.

The casket was lowered into the grave by straps which were operated by a little windlass. She had never seen that before. The mound of earth at the grave side was covered by a sort of rug with bright green artificial grass on it. She couldn't remember when she'd seen anything sillier.

Dr. Jackson was on vacation, or Muriel would have had him conduct the service. Ed hadn't expressed himself on the subject one way or the other and it would have meant a good deal to her to have a minister she knew. But she had no one else to call on except Dr. Jackson. So, she just let Jenny have the funeral parlor furnish the minister along with everything else. The one they hired looked all right; but as the casket was being lowered into the grave, he recited "The Lord is my Shepherd, I shall not want" in a voice that took her back to the Calvary Baptist Church in Dunreith—"the heavenly tone," as the Bells had called it—and she broke down at last and cried.

After the service, Gene drove Muriel and Jenny home to Twin Creek, first dropping Theda off at the supermarket where she clerked part-time and Shirley Ann off at the elegant ranch-style home where she was spending the summer as a mother's helper.

When they parked in the usual place in the yard, between the weeping willow and the ponderosa pine that had never done very well, Muriel told the two of them to go in ahead of her.

Jenny scrutinized her face. "You're sure you feel all right, Mother?"

"Yes, honey. I just want to sit here and think for a minute."

She watched them, broad and tall, walk to the house and up the three steps to the porch. Jenny was no heavier than she had been for several years—much too heavy, it was true, but still no more so—but Gene had put on a good fifty pounds in the past years. As he had said once to his father, "What do I do all day but sit in a car and drive around? The main exercise I get, heh heh, is hauling people out of wrecks." Then they'd got started on the technique of lifting corpses, and she'd disappeared into the kitchen. Both Gene and Jenny walked lightly; but they were young, their arches hadn't fallen yet. "Dear God, if it please Thee, spare Thou my children from the affliction of flesh which Thou has seen fit to bestow upon me."

She looked at this house where she had lived half of her life and from which she was being forced to move, and what she saw was a big brown shack in poor repair, redeemed from total dreariness by vines growing on it and by some dusty geraniums. She must sprinkle the flowers; they needed to be cut back; there was a lot to be done, weeding, cutting out dead wood.

She had just opened the car door when Jenny burst out of the house, screaming, "Dick! Mother, surprise, Uncle Dick is here!" Muriel said, "Oh good," to Jenny, but to herself she said, "At last. He's finally decided to come, has he." She walked toward the house slowly, so that when he stepped out of the front door onto the porch she would have to gaze up at him as though she thought he was something wonderful but with a set to her mouth that would let him know she didn't; she wanted to make him feel just how false his so-called superiority was. So independent all his life; high and mighty; going my own way, thank you very much. But he did not come even so far as the screened door to greet her. By the time she got to the living room she was seething.

She caught a glimpse of him on the couch, Gene at the foot

132

of it lighting a cigarette, Jenny coming in from the kitchen carrying a glass of something. "Well, Dick," Muriel began severely, but thank heaven she got no further. When she saw his sunken cheeks and blue lips the reproach died in her throat. "Oh, Richie, Richie, what is it?"

He tried to glare at her, then smiled. "They got me, Sis. They got me this time for damn sure."

"Everybody stay calm," said Jenny, "till his medicine takes effect."

She collapsed into the wicker chair. Her reserves were all gone. That futile glare of his had broken her heart. The last time she had called him "Richie" was the summer before he was to start in the first grade. She was about to go into the third grade, so of course she was not only much bigger than he but she had to see to it that he didn't get into mischief. For some reason that no one ever figured out, he had acquired the notion that Richie was a sissy name; he would only be called Dick from then on. For weeks, every time she called him Richie, he flew into such a tantrum that finally their parents, to humor him, obliged her to call him Dick. She did not dare call him Richie even on the sly as a threat to make him be good, because of his tantrums; their father always took his side against her on these occasions, though of course Mama was a little more realistic, knowing children for what they are, little angels with a streak of the devil in them. Now, here they were, well along in life, and she had harked clear back to their childhood without even intending to.

After a while he stirred, and Jenny propped his head up with a pillow.

"They tried to keep me in Honolulu, but I fooled 'em. My roving days are over. I didn't want to be put out to pasture so damn far from home."

"Complications?" said Muriel.

He nodded. "Heart."

"It's so wonderful to have you here again where I can look after you."

"Don't be a fool," he said.

"Dick!"

133

"You're in no shape."

"Who then? Roberta?"

Roberta was their older sister, married to a real estate operator in Kansas City. She had failed to send Muriel more than a Christmas card since sometime during the war, and Dick could not remember seeing her once since Mama's funeral.

"No, a convalescent home," said Dick, half-chuckling. "Convalescent home. It ain't a home, and you don't go there to convalesce. But that's where the action is, heh heh. What it is, is a dying house with hot and cold running water and nurses."

"Richard Storr!"

"I planned to hie me to Singapore where they got honest-to-goodness dying houses. No fooling. But here I am in Santa Rosa, so I got to make do with a convalescent home."

"There will be no more talk of this variety," she said vigorously. "Jenny, I don't know about you but I think it is time we had a bite to eat."

Gene surged back into action, and the house came to life again.

Dick poured himself a glass of wine to go with the meal. Muriel frowned.

"Isn't that bad for your heart?"

He raised his glass toward her mockingly. "Ashes to ashes, dust to dust, if the women don't get you the liquor must."

"I will *not* have such language in my house."

"Mother!" said Gene. "Doggone it, what's got into you?"

"I meant what I said. Besides, I was talking to my brother."

"When I get to the Great Beyond," Dick drawled, "I know who I'm going to find waiting for me there with a bar of soap in her hand—Mama. 'Richard,' she'll say, 'wash your mouth out this instant and never say a thing like that again.' For the rest of eternity I won't get to say what I want to, and there's nothing to do but grin and bear it. Well, believe me, Sister, on *this* side of the Great Divide, I'm going to say God-damn well what I feel like if I have to go to a convalescent home to do it. Shit. Shit."

Thinking he meant it, she gave up. If he was so stubbornly determined not to behave like a civilized human being, she would

134

not try to persuade him to come live with her in their declining years. So she just said what was on her mind—but not bitterly, for he was so shrunken and scrawny, his voice was so quavery, that her heart went out to him anyway.

"Oh, Dick, won't you ever grow up? You're still acting like a naughty little boy."

To her astonishment, she saw in the back-and-forth flickering of his eyes that right was going to triumph. Without planning to, she had succeeded—in fact, by planning not to. How strange.

Jenny, with Gene's bumbling goodhearted support, took charge and smoothed things over as only she could.

"This is a pretty kettle of fish," she cried. "Mother, time for your rest."

"A pretty kettle of fish"—the expression was unsuitable, but for that very reason it sounded all the dearer in Muriel's ears. It had been Mama's saying, which Muriel had kept alive, and now it was living in Jenny. Jenny too was saying it not because it meant much of anything but because it was her mother's.

"Well, by jiggers," said Gene, and though the phrase had not been Ed's exactly, it was *like* one of Ed's, "come on, Dick, let's have a game of checkers for auld lang syne."

Dick glanced at Muriel, and she beamed at him. "If you want to," he said to Gene. He sat up, adjusting a pillow to his back.

Muriel spoke to Jenny. "Well, honey, I think I'll just take my rest here. It's so comforting, on a day like this, to have my family about me. I want to watch the boys while they play." She settled into her corset. Dick was here for keeps. It was only a question, now, of working out details.

Dr. Bernard's glasses were making her vision much sharper, but it still was not all it should be. Once resettled, she would have to go back to Dr. Baum; he would send her to somebody reliable. Well, what could you expect from a girl doctor? Sometimes, as now, when she was inattentive or tired, she would begin to see double again, even with the glasses. It took great effort to bring the two images back together. It was easier just to let her left eyelid droop and see with only the right eye. Apparently watching the game of checkers, she practised closing her left eye

135

without bringing her right eyelid down far enough to obstruct vision, and also without squinting, so that other people might not be so likely to notice.

She left all the arrangements to Jenny and Gene. Ed had taken out a ten-thousand-dollar life insurance policy long ago when the hogs were doing well and had kept it up through the good times and bad—without so much as telling her about it till the last few weeks. That, Gene explained to her, plus something from the State plus Dick's benefits meant that she did not need to worry about money. Besides, he said one day, chuckling with embarrassment, "Don't fret, Mother, we'll take care of you, heh heh, no matter what."

Not far from where Gene and Theda lived, he found a house for rent, a stucco bungalow like all the others around—a tract house, whatever that meant—with no real yard, just some devil grass and a moth-eaten little hedge, but large enough for what they needed and with only one step. And Rosemary found them a Mexican grass widow with five children, Teresa, who would look after the house and help with cooking as Muriel needed.

Everyone was rallying round so wonderfully!

Strange, how little she regretted leaving Twin Creek Valley and the house where she had lived for upward of thirty years. It was not just Ed's passing, nor even the winery, really, though they certainly contributed a good deal to her state of mind. Friends: there was not a single woman, even in the club, she felt so close to that she would mind not seeing her regularly, not even Faith whom she had been seeing more often than anyone else these past years. And of course Santa Rosa wasn't *that* far away. And Faith promised to call at least once a week; her runaway son was settled in Santa Rosa now, the assistant manager in a branch of the Bank of America; she was thinking of moving into town herself.

"Faith Burger," Dick drawled. "Two faithburgers coming up, one with unction, one without."

"Now, Dick, Faith is one of the best friends I have in the world, and you must not play with her name."

136

"Excuse me, ma'am. Make that two without, and don't spare the sour pickles."

Three weeks after the funeral, she and Dick were ensconced —that was his word for it—in the new house, and Jenny was ready to fly back to Hawaii.

The afternoon before Jenny's departure while Dick was taking a nap, she told her mother her great secret: she was all but engaged.

"How wonderful, sweetie. Who is he?"

"A colonel in the Air Force. His wife is a hopeless alcoholic. She relapses every time."

"His wife?"

"Oh, he's divorcing her."

"I see." Muriel busied herself picking at the bedclothes. "I see. Alcoholic." She stared at Jenny's chin. "I'm sure that would justify divorce if anything could. Tell me all about him, honey."

Jenny said he loved her more than he had ever loved anybody else in his life and there wasn't anything she wouldn't do to make him happy.

For some reason, once they were settled in the new house, instead of feeling relieved or let down or whatever, she felt unsafe. Santa Rosa was completely familiar to her, of course, and she got around in it a certain amount still, shopping, going to an occasional meeting, visiting; yet she felt uncomfortable to be living in it. The noises at night were wrong; it was days before she knew where she was when she opened her eyes in the morning. The house itself she liked no more than Dick did, though she refused to join him in his complaining; all the same, it was so much like Gene and Theda's that she did not feel too strange in it. Yet, whenever she dropped her guard, she would realize she was feeling uneasy, not really safe.

It seemed to have something to do with her dieting. She had not needed to go back to Dr. Baum to decide, after Ed's passing, that she had better take herself in hand and drop some pounds. She had thought briefly of having a little contest with Jenny, to see which of them would lose more in the next six months, but she decided it might be wiser if she did it all on her own, without a word to anybody. She must not do it for praise or victory but because it was right. The pounds began to melt away, but their disappearance seemed to make her feel not so much satisfied and hopeful as increasingly vulnerable, unprotected.

Dick seemed to spend hours each day in front of Jenny's old TV set, but Muriel would get to feeling light-headed after half an hour of watching, maybe because she could do it with only one eye.

"So many informative programs."

"Yeah?" said Dick. "I'll say this much for TV, you get through a lot of time with it."

"And learn so many interesting facts."

"Nothing to stick to the ribs." He chuckled and patted the sides of his bony chest. Then he reached over and caught a roll of flesh under her armpit. "Keep watching, Sister, and some of this will quit sticking to your ribs too."

He was joking of course, albeit coarsely. All the same, this comment of his caused her to think about TV, about the odd feeling she had after watching it for any length of time, a feeling of loss which added to her uneasiness. Watching TV could not possibly make her lose flesh, though her weight continued to go down, at the rate of a pound a week. Still and all, she felt that it was causing her to lose *some*thing.

Teresa was working out very well, helpful, uncomplaining, playfully firm with Dick—a little slow to learn, perhaps, a little set in her odd Mexican ways, but hardworking and pretty clean. She was a Catholic, of course, so she wasn't really a grass widow. Her husband, Jesus, had returned to Mexico three years ago, to see his parents before they died, and she had not heard from him since, may God protect him. Grape-picking during the war, he had been accidentally knocked over by a truck and hit his head on a rock; he had not been the same after that and over the years had gotten worse slowly but steadily; it was God's will.

The one bad thing about Teresa was the casual way she would bring God into the conversation. For weeks, it made Muriel shift in her chair and pick at her dress to have someone

138

around who seemed to treat God like a member of the family. Teresa obviously had complete trust in Him. As Muriel of course did too. But she had never before known anybody who was *familiar* with Him. If she had been asked ahead of time, she would have said with conviction that it would be altogether wrong to be on familiar terms with the Almighty. But in Teresa, who was such a good and true servant of the Lord, it seemed altogether right. Muriel felt the more reproached by Teresa's piety because it was untainted with any reproach. She tried saying her prayers twice a day; but praying was not enough; things had changed; she let the matter slide. As for Teresa and God—those priests knew what they were doing; Teresa was so simple and childlike that naturally it made her feel better to think she had a wise, good father in the house. Truth to tell—though of course Muriel would never breathe it to a soul, except for Dick of course, and maybe Rosemary once in a while—Teresa was just a teensy-weensy bit slow in the mind; in fact, downright stupid.

That winter, Dr. Baum forced Muriel to begin taking medicine for her arteriosclerosis and to go on a terribly severe diet. But too late. In the spring her first serious stroke knocked her flat.

A week in the hospital, then another week in bed, tended by Teresa and Dick—yes, Dick rallied round and was more patient and helpful than anyone could ever have expected. Then she began getting up, if only to go to the bathroom—bedpans were so humiliating. Her balance was not what it had been, and her vision was permanently impaired; no matter how hard she worked to bring the two images together she could not. She walked slowly, touching furniture or the wall or holding some person's arm. But nothing seemed to be so paralyzed as to cripple her hopelessly.

She kept losing track of the days. The months lost themselves.

"I wonder which one Teresa is going to send tomorrow."

"Which one who?" said Dick.

"The good one or the bad one. Teresa."

"You mean you think there are two Teresas?"

She smiled indulgently. Her face was slack, she knew that from the way it felt and also from the mirror, but she still knew how to make her smile sweet.

"Three, Dick, not two. No no. The real Teresa stays at home. No mother," she explained to him as to a puzzled child, "would leave her children alone. For what? A dollar an hour?" She made a little dismissive *pftt* between her relaxed lips and rolled her head away from him on the back of the chair. "Usually she sends the good Teresa. A jewel. Such a good person. You just love her. Everybody does."

"Yeah, well, come on, Muriel, let's watch the giveaway show. They're getting started. Here, I'll put a glass of water by your right hand."

As he was setting the glass on the stand beside her chair, her hand darted out in slow motion and grabbed his arm before he could snatch it away; he was no quicker than she.

"Dick," she half-whispered, "she's in cahoots with Dr. Baum. That's why she sends the bad one whenever she can. They want to starve me to death. Help me. I'll let you know when."

"Come on, Muriel, forget it, nobody's going to starve you, I won't let them."

"I know you won't. You're such a comfort to me. We must be on our guard."

A respectable man with white hair and a young housewife with a silly grin on her face each went into a telephone booth and began answering questions about Alaska, the sort of odds and ends of facts Muriel had been reading in *Reader's Digest* forever. The winner had the choice of a baby elephant or a deep-freeze unit; the loser would get a hundred dollars.

"Why are they doing that, Dick?"

"Money. It's advertising. Corporations make money by giving it away, heh heh."

"But that's wicked."

"Atta girl, Sis, now you're talking."

"Why are we watching it?"

"It's as good a way to kill time as any."

"All right then."

She became aware of an anthology of poetry on her stand, *New Songs of Life*. Many of the poems were old favorites she was glad to recognize, and many she could not get interested in. But there were several she read again and again without bothering to understand, just because she enjoyed saying the lines over to herself. Reading them was the only thing she could do with one eye that gave her real pleasure.

> Grow old along with me!
> The best is yet to be,
> The last of life, for which the first was made.

A sweet thought. Robert Browning. Mama had been a member of a Browning Society for years.

> The best is yet to be . . .

What a lie. No, not a lie, a fib. So comforting. But did you ever in your life hear a bigger fib?

Gene bought her a special chair which she could adjust with a push or two, all the way from an upright position to one so reclining she could just sneak in a little catnap any time the spirit moved. So thoughtful of him.

He looked in on them every day without fail, at least for a minute or two, with a little story about something that had happened on the highway, or to see if they needed anything, really just to say hello. Theda seldom came by, which was just as well, but she sent little things to them by Shirley Ann two or three times a week.

Shirley Ann was such a well-behaved girl, soft-spoken, serious. Once in a while she would bring a friend by, and they would be giggly and self-conscious as girls should be. Her physical development was very pronounced; as her mother's had been at a similar age; maybe it went with a swarthy complexion and short legs to have an ample figure; or, more likely, it was the Indian blood. And the revealing clothes girls were allowed to wear these days, such tight T-shirts, such skimpy shorts. And the *suggestive* songs they listened to on the radio.

"Sweetie," she said to Gene, "I was having a chat with Shirley Ann yesterday—her little visits mean so much to me—and it turned out she didn't know who Samson was."

"Oh, hell, Mother, everybody knows he was a strong man."

"Yes, but that's not who he *was*."

"Maybe I don't know who he *was* myself."

"Oh, of course, you do, Genie. You went to Sunday school. We saw to that."

"A long time ago, Mother dear. Heh heh. It didn't stick."

"She should at least know about Delilah and what she did to him. Children need moral training. Bible stories. There are so many temptations besetting the modern world."

" 'Yield not to temptation,' " Dick croaked, " 'Dark passions subdue.' "

Gene and Dick broke up with laughing and tried to bully Muriel into a jolly mood. But she set her mouth and waited for them to calm down.

"Gene, you really should send her to Sunday school."

"Oh, yeah, well sure."

"I mean it."

"Come on, Mother, Theda and I don't ever go to church, and besides Shirl is nearly fifteen. It's too late."

"It's never too late to learn what's right."

"The world is changing. Sure, we want her to know what's right, for *her*, in the world of *today*."

"What's right never changes."

" 'Rock of ages, cleft . . .' "

"Richard Storr, stop that."

"Well, Mother," said Gene, "I've got to be running along now, Theda'll have dinner ready pretty soon, I'll be seeing you tomorrow sometime, let us know if you want anything."

"I do want something. I want to see that child taught her manners."

142

"Manners!" Gene cried.

"I sometimes think manners are the most important thing in life."

"I thought you were talking about morals."

"Morals, manners. Moral manners."

"Oh my God, what are you talking about?"

"Right and wrong. The way to live."

He took a deep breath, stubbed out his cigarette, and glanced at Dick, who winked. "Mother," he said in a gentle voice as he patted her arm, "leave her to me. Your system didn't work."

Her head rolled sharply away from him and her arm flinched. "Oh sure," she said with difficulty, "my system didn't work. Go away."

"Now, Mother, listen, damn it, don't get me wrong."

"Leave me alone, son." Her tongue was thick and heavy. "Go. Go."

For days, she talked only to keep people from noticing that she was not saying anything.

Teresa had just left after washing up the evening dishes.

"You heard what he said, Dick."

"Who? Stanley Garrett?"

"Who?"

"That guy," he said pointing at the screen. "The M.C."

"Will you please operate that infernal thing off."

"What the hell," he said with surprise. "Operate on it?"

"Cut out its brain, if that's what it has to cut out."

"I thought you liked these information shows."

"Pfft. I just said I did to keep from spoiling your fun."

He grunted. "So, now you want to spoil my fun."

"It isn't fun anymore, so how can I spoil it?"

"Okay, okay, I'll shut it off. Anyway, we need a new tube. There's too much snow."

> " 'Now is the winter of our discontent
>   Made glorious water by the sun of York.' "

143

"Wrong, Sis. I don't know what's right, but that's wrong."

"What's wrong? What are you jabbering about?"

"That quotation," he said shrugging.

"My son told me," she declaimed, "that my system didn't work."

"Neither does mine. We're a couple of old crocks."

"I am not a crock." Her voice was weepy.

"Oh, Jesus Christ, I meant: we're a couple of sick old folks."

She rolled her head away from him and spoke in a low voice. "He wasn't talking about our systems, you know that."

"I know it. If he had been you wouldn't be crying. So let's talk about what's wrong with us."

"Oh, Dick, what went wrong? What did I do wrong?"

"You ate too much."

She jerked around toward him and snapped, with the tears still glistening in her eyes, "Oh yes, I suppose you know so much about metabolism. The doctors don't, but you do. Bah."

"You asked me, I told you."

"My own son. And my daughter isn't even married, she doesn't have a baby, she'd be such a wonderful mother, she's just having fun in Hawaii."

"All right, she's having fun, she knows how to, anyway, she's good at it. What's wrong with fun?"

"My system didn't work."

"Doesn't work."

"Didn't work, doesn't work, never will work again."

Two mornings later, some sound made Muriel fight her way out of a laborious dream. It was a shriek from Teresa. She had found Dick dead in bed. He had died in his sleep, as he had always wanted to.

Muriel made herself go in and look at him. There was a faint smile on his lips, and his brow was smooth.

She became terribly confused, weary yet restless.

People came. She told them how thoughtful they were being.

The next day Jenny, when she arrived from Hawaii, gave a look around and said to Gene, "My God, why didn't you tell me?" She wrote two airmail special delivery letters, one to the sanatorium resigning her job, the other asking her best friend to ship her all her belongings. Muriel kept clinging to her, saying it had been so long.

"Too damned, long, Maw. You're right."

Jenny was fatter; her laugh was louder, harsher, not so jolly as it used to be; she smoked over two packs of cigarettes a day.

Teresa gravely assured Jenny, scrutinizing her eyes as she spoke, that there was a special corner in heaven reserved for good daughters. Muriel nodded, smiling.

"I bet there is," said Jenny laughing. "I just bet you there is, and all us good little girls are shoved off in it by ourselves."

"Get anything you want."

"Buttermilk chocolate creams?"

"You bet you Mike."

"Yummy."

"All you want."

"Isn't that sweet."

Muriel kept spreading and lifting her knees.

"Come on, Mother, put them down. It's sort of chilly and you knock the covers off."

"No."

"Yes."

"Why?"

"You'll get cold."

Muriel beckoned Jenny to bend over. "I'm going to have a baby."

"*You* are?" Jenny took a drag on her cigarette, looking at her speculatively. "No, you're not."

Muriel nodded. "I can feel it."

"You're just a crazy mixed-up kid, Mama, so keep the covers on."

"Don't say Mama." Muriel was severe. "Mama's dead."

"*My* Mama's alive and kicking."

"Oh yes." Muriel rolled her head away. "Sure, I know. You're just so jealous you don't want me to have any more ba-

145

bies." Then she turned back and poked Jenny in the abdomen. "Babies, babies, what's the matter with your babies?"

Jenny turned away suddenly; she stood staring at her burning cigarette. "Oh my God. What'll I do?"

"I know more than you think I do," said Muriel sluggishly but distinctly, "and you know more than I think you do."

Without taking a drag on the cigarette, Jenny watched the coal burn down to the filter, then stubbed out the butt long and thoughtfully. She turned back toward her mother, who, her left eyelid winking closed, squinted at her with the right eye. More than squinted at her: seemed to be seeing her.

"Cover me," she said in a large, yet not loud, voice. "Thou shalt not look upon the nakedness of thy mother."

"Yeah, okay, okay, it wasn't my idea. Stay covered up, you hear?"

"I'm going on a little trip, Mother."

"How nice for you, honey. Why?"

"I need a breath of fresh air."

"No, you don't. Where are you going?"

"Mexico."

"Jesus is in Mexico."

"Yah, sure, Jesus is everywhere."

"Jenny, *never* make fun of Jesus. Hay-soos. Teresas's Hay-soos."

"Hay-soos loves me, This I know, For Teresa tells me so."

"Such a sweet little song. It's been years since I heard it. Thank you, dear. So thoughtful of you."

"Are you being ironical, Mother? You can't mean it."

Muriel's gaze at her was blank.

"Anyway," Jenny went on, "you're in such good shape these days that I'm going to leave Teresa to take care of you, just five or six days. Dr. Baum is always available, and Gene is right around the corner."

"When?"

"Tomorrow."

Muriel clutched her to the bedside. "Bring me the vitamins."

146

"What?"

"Give them to me."

"Okay, but why?"

When Jenny put the bottle on the table beside the bed, Muriel laboriously reached over, took it, and slipped it into her bosom under her nightgown.

"Mother, what are you doing?"

"Where's Teresa?" she whispered.

"Out in back burning the trash."

"She'll be back in soon?"

"I suppose."

"Then I must hurry because she's the bad Teresa. You don't know it but she intends to starve me while you're gone. There was a scientist on TV—such a distinguished-looking man. He said you can live on nothing but water for days at a time *if* you have vitamins. It was one of Dick's programs." The back door slammed. Muriel looked furtively at the doorway to the kitchen, then closed her eyes. "Oh, how I miss him. How I miss my only brother. He meant so much to me. He was always so lively. Such good times we had. My childhood is gone. With him went my childhood."

"I'm sorry, Ma, but I've got to go pack up."

"Oh, sure, you're going too. They all go.

> 'Ding dong bell,
> Pussy's in the well,
> She's grown so stout
> She won't come out.
> Ding dong bell.'

Have a wonderful time, dear."

"My God, my God, my God."

"You wouldn't believe how bad I feel, Jenny. Head full of oatmeal mush. So hard to see anything."

"You see plenty, Mother."

"You can pull just so much wool over my eyes. Hah."

147

Faith dropped by for an hour or two every day Jenny was gone and kept Muriel in such good spirits, what with a game or an anecdote about some little event of her day or reading some pertinent article, that Muriel was reminded of the winter everyone had entertained her when she was laid up for five weeks with the grippe; she'd been fifteen. Rosemary came by on Tuesday afternoon, as she always did, and brought a potted azalea as a special treat. Mary Virginia Jackson "just happened" to be in town that Thursday and looked in to say hello. Theda sent a plastic doily by Shirley Ann—not too pretty with the garish clusters of grapes painted into it, but *so* practical. Apropos of nothing, Camille Piskor telephoned and gossiped for ten minutes.

Her resolve not to sleep day or night, while Teresa was in the house, was undermined the first day Jenny was gone: Teresa had sent neither the good nor the bad Teresa but had come herself. But in the middle of the seventh night Muriel woke up with an excruciating headache and had to ring. The bad Teresa came in, eyes narrowed, face black, demanding in a gruff voice, "What you want?" Muriel realized she must not give those claws an excuse to strangle her. In the sweetest voice she had, she apologized for being so much trouble and begged for aspirin. Teresa gave her a couple of white pills and a glass of water.

She lay awake, leaden with terror, waiting to see what the pills were going to do to her; their appearance had been so ominously innocent. They did nothing one way or the other, though at dawn she realized that the long vigil had made her headache recede. But the realization itself revived the ache. By breakfasttime, she was scarcely able to see even with the right eye. Fortunately it was the good Teresa who came to straighten the bed and soft-boil an egg for her. Muriel let go; now she could ask for aspirin tablets without anxiety and lie there confident they would do their work.

Shortly before lunch, Jenny breezed in, and Muriel startled out of a doze up into clarity.

"Oh, honey, back so soon?"

Jenny brayed. "Two days late, that's all."

148

"I hope nothing went awry."

"Good hoping, Ma. Everything's just hunky-dory."

Muriel saw for the first time how much Bell there was in Jenny's long face and steep forehead, how little Storr. There were tiny creases at the corners of her eyes and around her lips. She was going to be an old woman with a puckered mouth and squinchy eyes.

"I do hope you had a good vacation. I look forward to hearing all about it."

After Jenny had taken Teresa home, changed into shorts, served up lunch, unpacked, set the sprinkler on the lawn, done the dishes, called Theda to say she was back, and brushed her mother's hair, she sprawled in a chair and pumped a great sigh. "Hey, it's swell to be home."

"It's so good to have you." But Muriel had detected something odd in Jenny's tone, and she watched her carefully while seeming just to chat. "Do you know what Gene did a few days ago? He sneaked up behind me and put a patch over my left eye."

"The rat."

"Not only that, he glued it on."

"*Glued* it onto your *eye?*"

"No, you know, my pestacle." Her hand crept up to the left lens of her glasses. "I can't tell you how it annoyed me."

"Maybe he thought it would be easier if you didn't have to wink so much."

"And what if I like to wink?" said Muriel haughtily. It dawned on her what was odd about Jenny. "You're looking at something else."

Jenny shook her head. "Eh? How's that? I didn't hear right."

"Your eyes. They were staring at your big toe. Was that what you were looking at? No."

"No. Anyhow, I'm glad to see Teresa didn't starve you."

"Starve! It was all I could do to keep her from stuffing me with her tamales. They're so good. I'm a hog. Hot chicken tamales with those red hot peppers. Mm. You need a puppy."

Jenny was staring at her big toe.

149

"Jane! I said you need a puppy. A little dog."

"Right."

"What kind of a home is it that doesn't have the patter of little feet in it? And it will be several months before the baby is born."

Jenny jerked. Her face looked blasted. "How did you know?"

Muriel stared at her blankly.

"What baby, Mother?"

"I told you."

"Christ, can't you get babies off your mind?"

" 'To make the punishment fit the crime,' " she sang, " 'the punishment fit the crime.' "

"What crime?"

"I don't know, but oh, it must have been a terrible one. I was Pooh-Bah in *The Mikado.*

'My object all sublime,
I shall achieve in time—
To let the punishment fit the crime—
The punishment fit the crime.' "

Jenny sighed, deflating. "Did you enjoy being Pooh-Bah, Mother?"

"Pfft."

They were silent a long time.

Muriel spoke, even more slowly than usual, with stronger pauses, without slurring.

"Jenny, I honestly don't think I was so wicked that I deserve this much misery. Honestly."

"No, Mother, no one ever said you were wicked."

"So why is God punishing me so much? More than I deserve. There's only one reason: I'm a woman. If God had been a woman, I wouldn't be suffering like this. It was Father who always spanked me. Who makes wars? Men. Ed was a failure in life. I never told you that."

"Oh, yes, you did."

"I did not. I never said such a thing out loud before."

"Quit blaming so much, Mother. Casting blame."

"Don't interrupt. You make me lose my train of thought. Well, the important thing is, your father could have been a great singer, and he threw it all away. He had a beautiful natural organ. Everybody said so. Take Dr. Campbell—what kind of a man is he? He lets his wife cut his hair. Gene. One day Theda came here with a bruise on her forehead. She told me she'd run into a door, but Shirley Ann was with her and I could tell by her eyes—Gene did it. Men. They beat women. If only God weren't a man. If only. I wouldn't believe in Him if I could help it."

"You mustn't blame yourself so much."

"God is good. He can't be to blame. So I must be."

"Sweetie, what ever happened to Eileen Spratt?"

"Oh, I don't know. We've lost touch. Why do you ask?"

"You used to like her so much. Is she still in Santa Rosa?"

"The last I heard her husband ran off with an airline stewardess."

"Oh, but she was a Catholic," said Muriel with pain.

"She was," Jenny brayed, "but who knows what she is now? I got up to baptism myself, and look at me."

"Such a good nurse, Eileen. Wasn't she? Why don't you look her up?"

"I don't know. All in good time."

"You don't see people your own age. It must get so dreary for you here. It makes me feel bad. It's all my fault. How long has it been since you went to Mexico?"

"Three months."

"Just a movie once in a while, and Shirley Ann but she's not enough for you."

"I never went to Mexico."

"Oh yes, you did, for a whole week. But you didn't get to see Jesus."

"I started, but then I lost my nerve and turned around in midair."

"Bluck."

"Remember that J.C. basketball star I told you about, Ollie

151

Famosa? When he'd get near the basket, he would make a big beautiful jump, and right at the top of it he would stop and turn and shoot."

"Fiddlesticks."

"He did. I saw him do it. He was famous for it. Like a ballet dancer. Famosa. So I got way up in the air on the way to Mexico and all of a sudden I said to myself, 'I don't want to do that,' so I just turned around and landed in San Diego. I had a wonderful time, peachy. You know, lots of friends I hadn't seen for ages. Real fun."

"I'm so happy for you, dear—so much zest for life. Turn in midair? I could never have done that. Somehow, we took to singing in Ames, but we never danced very much. And now." She kicked one foot out from under the sheet, then closed her eyes.

"Want me to read some poetry to you, Mother? We haven't done much of that. It might be fun."

"You might just as well. 'The grave's a fine and quiet place.' I need some noise around here. I deserve it. Not even a little puppy. Read me that poem by Robert Frost. Such a wonderful nature poet. A lovely feeling for nature. About that witch with her son buried in the cellar and his bones come upstairs and knock on her bedroom door at night."

"Brr, it sounds grisly."

"I lost two babies, you know. Gene and you, and them. Wouldn't it be funny for a woman my age to have triplets? Funny-queer, not funny-haha. Mama's little joke." Tears began running from her eyes. "Oh, I do hope and pray I'm not hungry when they are born. Triplets. Quintuplets. God knows. Sextuplets even."

"Adoption. Jenny, what are you always dragging adoption into everything for?"

"I've been telling you, my friend in Hawaii. Don't you remember? I told you twice all about her. Her name is Jane, too."

"I thought she was an alcoholic."

"No, she had a withered leg."

"Oh yes, one of those."

152

"One of those? You mean, polio victims?"

"No no, withered friends. I had a withered friend. I know the type. Mona Tompkins; she married Roy instead. They had three perfectly normal children, two cute little girls and the handsomest boy. Fine friends you have. A colonel."

"He's the handsomest man I ever saw, Mother."

"You never saw your father sing 'Sheep may safely graze.' "

"I wish I had."

"You would have if I'd had my way. The way he held his head.—Adoption. So many mothers don't have children these days."

Jenny laughed painfully.

"You're laughing at me again."

"No, I'm not, Mother. It's just, some of the things you say are priceless."

"Thank you, dear, so good of you to say so. The point is, we simply don't have enough room in this house for any more children. It wouldn't be at all reasonable to try to. Besides, what would Rosemary think?"

"If there is one thing in this world I am sure of, it is that I don't give a hoot in hell what Rosemary thinks."

"Such language."

"Or Teresa. Or Faith Burger. Just you, Mama—what would *you* think?"

"Oh, honey, can't I get it through your head once and for all: Mama is dead. Please?"

"All right, all right. What would you have done if Gene and Theda hadn't ever got married and you learned that Theda had put Shirley Ann out for adoption?"

"It wouldn't kill me, if that's what you mean."

"That's not exactly what I meant, but it'll do. I'll tell Jane to keep the baby."

"There is much to be said for adoption," Muriel mused. "The agencies are so conscientious. A child needs a father. It's nature's way."

"But does the father need the child? That doesn't seem to be our way."

Suddenly Muriel's head began to roll back and forth in torment. "'Mother, your system doesn't work.' My own son said that to me." She squinted at Jenny balefully. "My own son."

"I know he did, Mother. We don't have to dwell on it."

"Oh, yes, we do. And he isn't even man enough to smoke a cigar. Makes him choke. Hah! Filtered cigarettes."

"If that's the worst thing to be said about him . . ."

"It's not. As you are well aware. Where's that squealing come from?"

"My rocking chair. Or else one of the floorboards."

"The dearest little piggy in the world. His mother ate all the litter but him. Ed called her a devil-sow, and he was right. He was so often right. I fed him on a bottle but he drowned. I wasn't a good enough mother to him." Slowly, inaccurately, she wiped her eyes. "So sad. 'Tears, idle tears, I know not what they mean.' We must take her babies from her as soon as she farrows, Jenny. She might eat them. Sows do."

Jenny stood beside her and stroked her forehead. "Here I am, Mother."

Muriel gazed at her unresponsively for a few moments, then made a little smile, lips trembling. "So good to me. More than I deserve."

ABOUT THE AUTHOR

George P. Elliott is Professor of English at Syracuse University. Born in Indiana and a graduate of the University of California, he has also taught at the University of Iowa, St. Mary's College in California, Cornell, and Barnard College. His previous books include three novels, two short-story collections, two collections of essays, two college textbooks, and a book of poetry.